Praise

"Shy's disordered, multidimensio[n...] Max Porter's brief and brilliant [...] hapless, hurting child and a dangerous, violent young man, and his author has loved each part of him into being with the same steady attention."

—**Hermione Hoby,** *The New York Times Book Review*

"Sublime. . . . What a miracle of language this book is. . . . With *Shy*, Porter has not only equalled but surpassed the triumph of his debut." —*The Irish Times*

"[*Shy*] exists in a fascinating liminal space: a painful and unexplored past and an uncertain future. Porter is at his finest here."

—**Michael Welch,** *Chicago Review of Books*

"Slim, potent. . . . What [*Shy*] wants . . . is to capture the sensory experience of living for a few hours inside Shy's throttled mind. . . . The feeling of identification pays powerful dividends at the novel's cathartic ending." —**Sam Sacks,** *The Wall Street Journal*

"There are few writers who can explore the psyche—and also the limits of language to describe it—with the lyricism and economy of Max Porter."

—**Miranda Collinge,** *Esquire* **(UK), "Best Books of 2023"**

"Max Porter's books are always as much poetry as they are prose; they are tiny works of art that never fail to move and engage."

—*Literary Hub*, **"Most Anticipated Books of 2023"**

"*Shy* is . . . written out of love for its bewildered subject. It offers a challenge to recognize the complexity of the difficult road faced by boys like Shy, as well as to understand them complexly—to see both their struggle and their joy, to meet them where they find themselves, and to help lighten the load."

—**Joel Pinckney,** *Los Angeles Review of Books*

"Hugely readable, even gripping. . . . It is virtuoso."

—**Kevin Power,** *The Guardian* **(UK)**

"Stylistically unorthodox, a little mystical, with a big heart and a small page count. . . . The narration unfolds as a kind of spectral swirl of voices. . . . Vivid scenes erupt like lightning in fog."

—**Anthony Cummins,** *The Observer* **(UK)**

"His most beautifully-wrought writing to date, an ode to boyhood and a sensitive deconstruction of rage, its confused beginnings, its volatile results, and all the messy thoughts in between. . . . Porter's writing is warped transgressively across the page, but also deliciously rich. . . . The book balances these deeply social-psychological themes with charmingly—sometimes hilariously—candid moments. . . . A true triumph." —**Izzy Smith, The Arts Desk (UK)**

"Porter has already developed a body of work distinguished by its concision, poetic facility of language and polyphony, in novels that also pack a devastating emotional punch. . . . *Shy* is an act of humanity and grace, heightened by its distinctive form and artistry."

—**Luke Kennard,** *The Telegraph* **(UK)**

"With masterly economy . . . [Porter has] created a fragile character on the edge of sanity yet alive to the beauty of the natural world."
—Claire Lowdon, *The Sunday Times* (UK)

"Max Porter writes incredible things. They're generally short, poetic, exquisitely executed tales of tragedy shot through with beauty. . . . [*Shy* is] incredible, brutal, crude, sad and absolutely stunning."
—Louise Ward, *The New Zealand Herald*

"*Shy* is an intervention, a warning, a dazzling bolt of prose in the long night of our times."   **—Max Liu, inews.co.uk**

"The question of sympathy is not the only focus of *Shy*. A story about an alienated, angry teenage boy is, of course, also a story about masculinity and male socialization. And *Shy* addresses elements of this process that tend to be ignored."
—Rachel Connolly, *The New Republic*

"A wholly unique, affecting portrait of a troubled teenage mind desperately trying to outpace its own intrusive thoughts. The end result is messy, but that seems to be the point. There's no one writing books quite like Max Porter."
—Michael Knapp, *The Adroit Journal*

"A worthy fourth novel by a master craftsman and artist."
—John Slayton, *New York Journal of Books*

"In language that shimmers, rages and churns, Max Porter has once again written an unparalleled masterpiece."   **—Lucas Rijneveld**

SHY

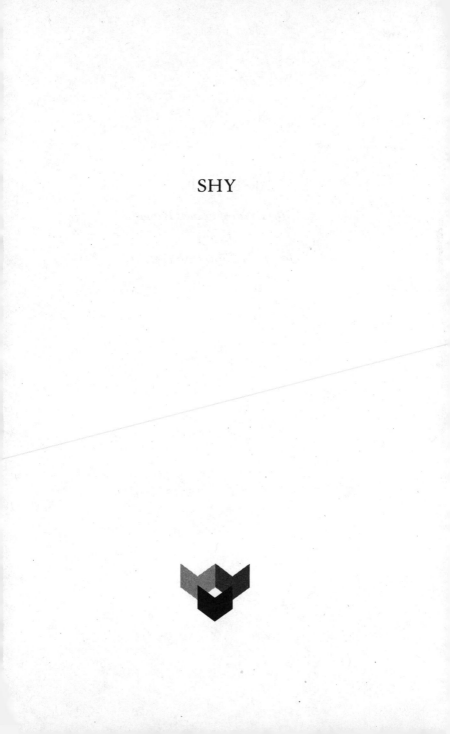

SHY

A Novel

MAX PORTER

Graywolf Press

First published in 2023 by Faber & Faber Limited, London

This publication is made possible, in part, by the voters of Minnesota through a Minnesota State Arts Board Operating Support grant, thanks to a legislative appropriation from the arts and cultural heritage fund. Significant support has also been provided by other generous contributions from foundations, corporations, and individuals. To these organizations and individuals we offer our heartfelt thanks.

Published by Graywolf Press
212 Third Avenue North, Suite 485
Minneapolis, Minnesota 55401

www.graywolfpress.org

Published in the United States of America
Printed in Canada

ISBN 978-1-64445-229-5   (cloth)
ISBN 978-1-64445-289-9   (paperback)
ISBN 978-1-64445-230-1   (ebook)

2 4 6 8 9 7 5 3 1
First Graywolf Paperback, 2024

Library of Congress Control Number: 2023951382

Cover design: Carlos Esparza

Cover image: Fernando Lavin

For Lisa Baker

Up and at 'em, Shy.

The rucksack is shockingly heavy.

The floorboards complain.

He checks again: the spliff is diagonal-snug in the empty Embassy box.

The daytime check is a half-dream away.

The room is molten soft. Tempting.

Jumpy.

The rucksack is shockingly heavy.

It's 3.13 a.m.

It's a full bag of rocks, of course it's heavy.

> *The average flint is about 600 million years old, said Steve.*

Snapping point. Creaking straps.

Walkman ready.

Pandemonium *Andromeda Tour*, Plymouth 1994, Tape 1.

Randall back2back Kenny Ken.

> *Express how you're feelin.*

Jungle.

The pinnacle.

The Amen.

Almighty.

A way of life.

Big hot and heavy.

600 million years, and we think we're tough lasting one hundred tops. He can't hold it still in his head.

Size.

Butterflies in his tummy.

Time.

Slightly needs a shite.

He leaves the room dark. Shy's room minus Shy. *Eve 1965* carved in the beam. A wonky heart carved in the beam. *1891* carved in the beam. *Shy 95*, fresh and badly scraped in the beam, with a jagged S like a Z. Couldn't even get that right.

The future is here, Shy. It's yours.

He stays in the middle of the carpet down the corridor to avoid the squeak.

Jamie never sleeps, but he'll have his headphones on. Steve, Amanda, Owen downstairs, Benny, Posh Cal, Paul, Riley, Ash.

The rucksack is shockingly heavy.

Sneaky little dickhead.

His shoulders are killing him.

One step then another.

Easy does it.

Smell the chilli con carne from earlier.

Armpits and food carpets farts.

Your mum.

Tex-Mex and old-damp stone.

He stops at the bottom and nibbles on his thumbskin.

Shwooshtick-Shwooshtick, the electric meter like a slowly rewound break.

Caught between times. In the fold. Escaping.

Little Shy at thirteen o'clock with the last of his skunk and his favourite tape. Boy on the stairs, stepping through. *Tom's Midnight Garden*. That's what it feels like, fuckinell that's exactly it. He hasn't thought about that book for years.

'This is Shy. He's usually to be found here, in the snug, with his headphones on, chatting to himself.

If the straps go then it's game over, a hundred flints
clattering on the flagstones at the foot of the stairs.
Listed stairs, listed floor, listed history, pissed-off
teachers.

Shitty Reebok rucksack he's had forever.

Lynx Africa.

His heart is bomp-bomp-bomping like he's scared.

Idiot drama with no audience. Overthinking
overlapping voiceovers.

> *We made such good progress today, Shy. I'm really
> delighted.*

He's sprayed, snorted, smoked, sworn, stolen, cut,
punched, run, jumped, crashed an Escort, smashed
up a shop, trashed a house, broken a nose, stabbed his
stepdad's finger, but it's been a while since he's crept.
Stressful work.

'Psychologically disturbed juveniles requiring
special educational treatment, or a bunch
of teenage criminals on a taxpayer-funded
countryside retreat?'

6

He's through to the conservatory, carpet-quiet nine careful steps to the tall window behind the skanky floral curtain. This'll be some posh twat's kitchen next year. The old windows don't open. The newer windows, sixties upgrades, open nice and silent. He steps out of the musty house and puts his hood up.

[The camera pans across the lawn.]
'An ordinary bunch of teenagers kicking a ball about, or some of the most disturbed and violent young offenders in the country? Here at the unconventional Last Chance school, it's reiterated time and time again: they can be both.'

He could jog, to be out of view faster, but the stones would be noisy, so he keeps on creeping. He peers back at the house and thinks of them all in there. Tucked up. Owen and the overnight staff and the boys. Out for the count til alarm, guffing and breathing and dreaming of whatever stressed or violent or sweet and easy shit they dream of. Everyone always says they sleep mad deeply here. New kids talk about their fucked-up dreams and then the ghost stories do the rounds (Mrs Nash who watches over you while you're sleeping and sips your nightbreath; the skinny old man in the nightie who walks up and down the back stairs dripping piss) and the true story of Sir Henry Radcliffe who murdered a servant in the top locked bedroom and that's why everyone hears a scream when they first move in, dead of night, a single scream, a welcome to the house from its own traumatised past. Everyone's heard it, and if they haven't they pretend.

> *For such a clever boy, you really are intent on crashing your own train, aren't you?*

The night is huge and it hurts.

> *Chippy little twat all of a sudden, aren't you? Thought you were depressed?*

He turns his back and wanders into the blue. Moving shadow.

Last year, still at home, still at normal school, when he went to Becky's at lunch and he was fiddling around trying to get the smelly greasy-thick condom on, useless knob like a dumpling, numb, Becky being sweet and too helpful, gently caressing, flopping it side to side and squeezing, trying an awkward semi-blowy, pity smile, looking at it like it was hurt, poor sad willy, which made it worse, so he got dressed, didn't say anything, wasn't nice, stormed off red and untucked, Becky asked him to stay, to chill, skin up, relax, not make it into a big deal, but he thumped downstairs embarrassed and tearful, left Becky's house ashamed, stormed back to school and thought if life was this much stress, this much pressure, it's too much, it's too fucking much, the whole thing is hassle, how does anyone deal with it, Becky being sweet, shame into anger, tethered to the last mistake, everyone waiting for the next one, never be sat in a tidy clean room with a nice person listening, thinking of something they want to hear, occasional stretches of fine, sat inside time's strict channel, just being alright, pissing about, sometimes fun then back in a hole, all the damage, then the inescapable atmosphere of having fucked up, tilted back to square one, rigged, Becky's sad face looking at his little beige dick shrinking, foreskin bunched like a mole rat, like a traitor, after all that raging horn, all the nice snogging, learning to lick her, boners galore, sticky boxers and chapped lips and god he wants to curl up and sob, all the handjobs in the rec, all the *waiting til we're ready*, such a typical let-down, he always imagines how things will be and gets upset when they don't work out exactly like that, now he's got double chemistry, of all the lessons, bad mood aggravator, the smell of the lab, Mrs Fryn getting on his tits, wishing he could go back, rewind operator, back to the brag, the excitement, the tingles, the school is taunting him, endless stairs, long corridors, missed the bell, still got his V-plates, barged into the science wing, threw his bag on the floor of the chemistry lab and started chatting shit to Noddy, and Mrs Fryn said *I don't think I like your attitude* and he said I don't think I like your face and she told him to leave and see the head immediately and he said Actually fuck you and as he walked out he dragged an arm along and brought one, two, three, four, five whole chemistry kits smashing down, glass flasks and pots of acid and metal clamps and Bunsen burners, and there was nothing but gasps and giggles from his lab-coated classmates and he walked straight out of school, lit a fag on his way across the playground, guessed today was probably the final straw as far as the school was concerned and knew he'd have to sit and listen to his mum's snotty repetitive questions all evening, *But why, but what possessed you, are you hearing me, what's going on with you, why are you doing this to me, speak to me, to us,* his stepdad leaning in the door giving him judge-eyes, fucking self-important twat, so he headed for Gill and Michael's house, they left a key under the mat for him and if things ever got too much he was allowed to sit in their smart kitchen and decompress, friends of his mum and stepdad, never had kids of their own, maybe Gill's his godmother, he can't remember, he lets himself in, paces around their kitchen for a bit muttering, eats a load of custard creams, looks at their stuff, Gill and Michael in Paris, Gill and Michael in Corfu, a framed poster saying *99% CHANCE OF WINE*, a calendar with garden birds, he opens their drinks cabinet and has a swig of Gordon's, then he smokes a fag on their patio, pacing, wishes he still had that whizz from Fantazia, then he has a glass of vodders, then he finds some cans of Kronenbourg in the fridge and glugs one down, then he has some more vodka and lies on the sofa in the conservatory, then he has another can of beer and smokes a fag, then he hears the front door open so he slams the door to the kitchen shut, wonders what to do, hears Gill make a scared little *oh* sound, picks up a chair, smashes the glass cabinet with all the fancy wine glasses in, hears Gill shriek, hears the front door slam, starts on the photos, punching glass, Gill and Michael at Avebury hugging a stone, Young Gill on a balcony

11

looking sunburnt, punches the whole wall of pictures fast and hard like the game at the fair whacking pop-up heads, knuckles bleeding, one deep cut with a tiny cube of glass embedded, smashes the wine poster, yanks the microwave out of the socket and chucks it on the floor, smashes the bottle of vodka against the wall, wallops the conservatory door with the chair but it's reinforced glass so the leg of the chair just breaks, he screams once, a loud crackled yelp, drops the broken chair, sits on the sofa and starts crying, hiccuping, shit, grrrrr, fuck, starts to feel a little bit better and by the time the sirens come he's feeling calm, and sort of sorry.

He stops on the edge of the lawn, where Jamie kicked Nick Fulshaw's head in last term and the police kept asking why nobody saw him lying there bleeding and everyone said again and again *Because of the ha-ha*.

Shy's mum phoned and said they were worried about him and he should be careful, smoking so much, perhaps it's stunting his growth, can't be good staying indoors all day, sitting around listening to his drums and bass, and he told her he loved drum n bass much more than he'd ever loved her and then he hung up.

The memory is camouflaged with other shitty things.

He called her back.

Nice chat, you fucking whiny old bint. Don't bother next time. Just leave me alone. Tell Iain Piss off from me.

He hung up again, leaving the sound of her sob in the handset.

He looks back and the house is like a fuzzy old photo with all the colours drained. He half expects to see a pale face at the window.

Good riddance, boys.

Peace out, ghosts.

Bm-psh – bm-psh

bm-psh – bm-psh

his spitty internal beatbox,

walking in time,

step by darkstep nod and step,

one, two, *gumf*, *click*,

palate snare,

throat kick,　　　sneaking away from the Last Chance.

[Amanda, senior live-in staff member,
comes from a background in social care and
thrives on the challenges of this progressive
educational environment]
'Imagine a stage, a few badly paid backstage
staff, and a troupe of highly unreliable and volatile
actors. Young male actors with very complex
backstories. Tragic stories, in some cases. It's a
ruddy cosmic miracle we ever get through a single
night. A magnificent fluke. So yes, they can sell
this old place to the highest bidder but it won't
undo the work we've done here.'

They talk a lot. More than any of them ever have before. Sometimes with the teachers, unpacking what they've been through, what they've done, just chatting in lessons, or in little groups, sudden moments of honesty. Jamie told them about when he got his diagnosis aged thirteen and all his mates stopped talking to him. His best friend started calling him a retard. *I won't ever forgive that*, said Jamie. Everyone agreed, that's unforgivable. *Not as long as I live*, said Jamie. Benny talked about his dad dying in prison. He almost cried and everyone was silent while he got his shit together because Benny is the toughest and nobody ever sees him cry. Paul talked about what he'd done and his time in borstal and how he'd lost his virginity when he was eleven and they didn't feel easy making sex jokes around Paul after that, but Paul mostly stays in his room playing his SNES. They tell stories. Some bragging, some regret, some baffled grinning shrugs and ripples of easy laughter. They talk about how wrong school was for them. They try and figure each other out, because there's fuck-all else to do. They each carry a private inner register of who is genuinely not OK, who is liable to go psycho, who is hard, who is a pussy, who is actually alright, and friendship seeps into the gaps of these false registers in unexpected ways, just as hatred does, just as terrible loneliness does.

His mum has written down: *Like a person being devoured / animal that's in him / skin ? on him / trapping him / Shy's inside, but the skin is also him, so angry, so true. I'm almost envious.* And Jenny says *Gosh. This is so interesting. Thank you.*

And Jenny says *Shy? Anything you want to share? Just a doodle today, is it?*

And Jenny says *Sorry, I'd hoped this would be a helpful thing.*

And Jenny says *It's alright, sometimes you can say nothing.*

And Jenny says *Shy?*

If someone looked out of the window he'd only be a head. *Because of the ha-ha.*

He waits by the hedge and nibbles his fingers and thumbs for a minute, chewing through burning memories, spitting chunks of skin and nail into the dark.

He sits up from deep sleep into the blood-orange dim-ness of his childhood room, lit by the landing light outside, and sees a red-dark featureless animal crawl-ing slowly across the bedroom floor towards him, dragging something lifeless and lumpen behind it, sniffing, creaking and snuffling, bringing him a dead thing, coming in, a nightmare-hungry dog or half-man killer, but the room is real and he feels his duvet cover to check, touches his face, scratches his hair, and then with a resigned grinding of mental gears his fear turns to disappointment as his eyes and mind align and help him understand that this nocturnal beast is Iain, it's Christmas Eve, this is his stocking being very carefully left at the foot of his bed, this is crinkling packaging noise mixed with Iain's heavy breath and clicking joints and those pointed ears emerging at the foot of his bed are the Batman mask he asked for, poking out from the top of the tightly stuffed giant sock, and of course he has heard the playground rumours and he has had his doubts for a while, but he is wondering why it makes him so sad to have it finally confirmed – he still gets the same presents, after all – but he is surprised Iain is making so much noise, that he is so unsubtle, spoiling the magic of Christmas, so Shy lies crossly back down and waits for Iain to leave, but Iain starts cussing in a posh girly voice so Shy sits up again and dimly perceives that Iain is the girl dressed in old-fashioned clothes, her again, the girl in the knitted jumper, and she's unpacking his stocking and throwing his presents across the room, taking swigs from a bottle of clear spirits, and the room is huge, his posters are gone and his bed is against a different wall, and he starts to smile because this keeps happening, this one dream un-waking into another dream, he's ten years older and fucking fast asleep and dreaming in the Last Chance, this is the girl who mutters in the walls between his room and Paul's, and the girl is furious, unpacking all his toys because she doesn't want a six-year-old's rubbish, baffling crap from the future, she's stamping on cars and action figures, making a hell of a noise, doesn't want his Skywalker toothbrush, doesn't want his pack of Asda socks or his Ninja Turtle Pez machine, she is flinging things as hard as she can across the room, she chucks his satsuma on the floor and stamps it splat as the light shocks on and Shy's mum and stepdad are standing in the doorway asking *What the hell*, and Shy is blinking, can't see a thing, can only hear them, *What in the ever-loving fuck are you doing, boy*, *Oh god poppet why would you do this*, *You bloody spoilt little monster*, and Amanda is knocking on the door which is suddenly right by his head, saying *Is everything OK in there, Shy? I'm coming in, Shy, I'm coming in on the count of three, ready, one, two, three*, and Shy is keeping his eyes closed, waiting, trying desperately to be gone before Iain comes in, yearning to be asleep, because if he wakes up he's spoilt everything, if he wakes up he'll have to start answering.

Camera-shy. Haha, well exactly, not so Shy after all. He'll need a new nickname. He's really found his feet in the group. It's a shame he doesn't want to be in the programme. He'll change his mind, I bet. Once Cal or Benny get involved.

His cousin Shaun hasn't picked up when he's called him recently. It's been ages. Maybe he's got a new number or he's not living in the same place. He's called him twenty, thirty times. He sits in the phone room, stewing, imagining reasons.

They went to London for the day, him and Shaun. To Black Market Records. Shaun who got him into jungle. Shaun who lent him magazines and let him use his decks. Shaun who drove him to the car park behind the rec every Saturday and shared little lines of coke on the dashboard while they listened to mixtapes. Shaun whose *hee-haw* smoker's laugh Shy's been trying on for size. Shaun in the busy commuter train to London being bouncy and loud *Big up all small-town lads, Shauny and Junior Shy on the rampage, am I right am I fucking riiiight bidder bang bidder bang bidder bang, hold tight the man big up the plan.* On a pilgrimage to the city. Overexcited. Jumped the barriers on the Tube. Nicky Blackmarket was behind the counter in the shop. They asked for extra plastic bags. Hall of fame. *These are the days.* Remember the days.

It feels ridiculous to be stood in the garden in the dark with this stupid rucksack yanking his shoulders off. Like a twatting Cub Scout.

Shy said It's our music, coming out of our shit towns, it's not from Staten Island or Seattle or Detroit, it's from Walsall and Watford.

Shaun and his mate Andy burst out laughing and Andy did a squeaky voice and said *Fwom Wycombe and Weading and . . . Wochdale* and Shy said Fuck off Andy, and Shaun said *Argh man, learn to take a joke, yeah?*

Failed 11+. Expelled from two schools. First caution in 1992 aged thirteen. First arrest aged fifteen. Is this you? The whole of you? You've got to work your arse off to lose this piece of paper. I won't have any of you lads defined by what you've done in the past, but you'll have to put the bloody work in. There's no magic switch we can flick. Are you hearing me?

He does his breathing exercise on his fingers, one-two-three. Come on, you pussy.

He walks through the gap in the hedge and into the bottom garden. He's trespassing through a freeze-frame. It's colder down here. Paused, threatening.

He thinks of the time in Year 8 when he was walking home from school across the rec and he had his head down, scuffing the grass, talking to himself, unselfconscious, interviewing himself about why he'd like to play the part of Joseph in *Joseph and the Amazing Technicolor Dreamcoat*, and two older girls, chain-smoking sixth-formers, fully grown women, were suddenly next to him, ripping the piss, slumped along impersonating his walk, his daydream, *I really feel that as a billy no-mates I could really imagine loving my coat of many colours*.

He plods along, heavy-footed, alert.

> *If things are closing in, go to one of your Cheery Thoughts.*

He imagines arriving in a club and heading to the booth, white labels in his bag, crowd parting to let him through, fist-bumps, huge blunts, free drinks, *Yes boss*, *Big up*, *Respect*.

Amanda: *Tell me about it.*
Shy: I was in a mood. Iain was lecturing me about my behaviour, and I saw his hand, I was cutting up a carrot, and before I know it the knife is stood upright in his little finger and everyone's angry with me. God knows why.

Amanda: *You shouldn't joke.*

Shy: Me and him ended up bonding over it a bit, actually. He didn't press charges. He can be alright. Anyway it only chipped the bone. He's got chubby fingers.

The lower garden is brambly and wild. They clear it sometimes and it grows right back. It grows back fast.

Troubled little plants growing in the English scrub, but you're worth saving, aren't you? Put your hand on your heart and tell me that you don't feel energised and pleasingly tired and a little bit educated, out here, in the fresh air?

He talked to himself while he worked in the garden because they weren't allowed headphones. Chatted crap and mumble-rapped. Find me the bindweed fine weed bind to the mind weed all the time never mind leave me behind weed. Yanking up great thick lengths of tangled root, stubborn leaves and little white umbrellas. Talking to himself since he was a kid.

First sign of madness, said his nan.

Nettles. Dandelion. Bugloss. Brambles. Steve is teaching them as they hack away. *Morning glory*, and they all laugh.

Shy vs Goosegrass: Dillinja remix. Plantain. Dock. Toxic shock. Chop chop chop. Witness how Bindweed Babylon faaaaaaaalls, mutherfuckaaaa, Shy screamed as he grabbed and pulled, and the others all laughed with him.

Last view of the house from the bottom hedge.

The ghost of Lady Nash or whatever. *Bon Voyage, Shy.*

Later, wankers.

When he was nine and Mark and Lizzie Bailey came for dinner and they brought their son Toby for a sleepover and the kids stayed up late watching cartoons and had Friday Sweets and Toby had the Z-bed on the floor and they talked until they were told off and then they whispered until Toby got sleepy and then Shy got up and tried to find his Ewoks to show Toby but it was too dark so he got back into bed and then they talked some more and Shy got up to try and find his Garbage Pail swapsies but it was too dark and he trod on Toby who squealed and said he needed to go to the loo but Shy heard Toby go down the stairs so he tippy-toed after and sat on the bottom step and listened while Toby said he wanted to go home and his parents asked why and Toby said he didn't really know he just wanted to go home and Iain said *You can be honest, did he upset you* and Toby said *No, I just want . . .* and Lizzie said *He just likes his own bed*, and Iain said *We're getting more and more of this kind of behaviour*, and Shy heard his mum say *Iain I don't think . . .* and Iain said *He doesn't really know how to socialise with others, you know, classic only child*, and Shy heard a chair scrape so he barefoot-bolted up the stairs and into bed and heard his mum's soft step across the landing, into his room, the weight on the end of his bed, a hand on his leg, he kept his eyes pretend-sleep shut, *I know you're awake, love, I know you can hear me, it doesn't matter, we can try*

25

again, maybe Toby isn't grown-up enough for sleepovers yet, it's not your fault, and she did his favourite wafting-the-duvet trick and went back down and Shy lay prickly wide awake, listening to the grown-ups leaving, plates and glasses, *Don't worry leave all that*, coats and shoes and Mark saying *Gutted to miss that dessert, better get this one home*, Iain saying *Sorry again about you-know-who*, Lizzie saying *God not at all, I think just a case of too much sugar and a very late night, we can try again*, and Shy's mum saying *Yes, please, let's definitely try again.*

Please don't start the day telling us what y

speaking to us / If you think that's an OK

to have a serious think / Why are you do

control / This is not normal / You need to

/ This is not OK / I can't believe you are

nice, ruin a family day out, congratulatior

are words coming out of my mouth / Wl

in? / What is going on in your head? / I

understand, totally unacceptable / Talk to ι

/ How dare you speak to us lik

ɔu don't want to do / Listen to how you're

way to speak to your mum then you need

ng this, today of all days? / You are out of

get a grip of yourself / You cannot do this

doing this / What a way to behave / Oh

s / Well, young man, I'm appalled / There

y do you want to hurt us / Hello, anyone

o you get it? / It's unacceptable, do you

s / Talk to us / Talk to us / Woah calm down

that / Enough / Get back here

He might topple off this night-edge and scurry back to bed.

Lavender capsules, whale music, story tapes, Rescue Remedy, breathing, SSRIs, regular exercise, his diary, his walks, and now his mum's read an article about St John's wort, so she's sending him a little bottle, drop a spot in your tea every morning, plop a drop in each eyeball, stab yourself in the heart with John's worty blade, clamber up on St John and have a ride, aren't you better yet? Aren't you fixed? Aren't you having lovely dreams? Aren't you ready to go to college, then to uni, get a job, get married, have kids?

Benny is taking the piss out of Steve and Shy tells him to shut up.

You what, short-arse? says Benny.
I said, Shut up, says Shy.

The whole room tenses, the collective intake of breath before a ruck.

Benny gets up and walks over.
Shy clenches, ready for a slap.

Watch yourself, faker, says Benny, and flicks Shy's forehead.

He could turn back and be tucked up in bed in five minutes.

Is it ever exhausting, being you?

His thoughts are lopping along in odd repetitive chunks, running at him, stumbling. Feels brave, feels pathetic, feels nothing. Panic. Calm. Mad clatter in the roof of the break like machine guns then swirling calm, home, school, years ago, yesterday, his mind all tight, then slackening, then something buzzing under like a tectonic plate, then marching, then pure noise, then snapping traps, then humming, bassline in his migraine, under the bathwater private time, then a dancey synth part in the clear sleepless noise of his insomnia, piano choon, one step forward two step backward, building a real thing, into the movement, which is like, oops, slippery on the leaves here, haha nearly went down.

Shaun laughed at Shy's bedroom. Flyers for clubs he's never been to. Sleeves Blu-tacked to the wall but no turntables to play the records on. Logos stencilled and sprayed.

Time must be passing. Weight, rhythm, music for people too self-conscious to dance, just stand still and nod, stand still and step, fall over, get up, wake up, Shy keep walking. Where your mates at? Go it alone. Shy Guy, far from home. Nearly at the fence, remembering tension, remembering hassle, keeping it tight on a leash in his head.

> *Wow. It's like when you were absolutely fuckin obsessed with dinosaurs. Then Hot Wheels and Micro Machines and that. Now you're like a stalker for jungle, haha, only kidding mate, safe, safe, you're alright.*

The night is huge and it hurts.

> *Hurry up and slit your wrists. Nobody likes you, teacher's pet.*

He replays the days; was he lame, was he cocky, was he keeno? Has he missed a joke? He falls asleep judging himself with no context. In his dream he's offended someone, then everyone, then he's hunted and taunted so he stabs through the fence, stabs naked backs, stabs soft temples and vulnerable gaps. In his dream he is smashing Posh Cal's head on a sharpened metal fencepost and leaving him gasping, gurgling red, then he is swaggering tight in a posse, wide awake fixating on social dips and troughs, safety and risk, failed gags, piss-takes, sometimes awake, mostly in between shit feelings and murder dreams and wanking til his knob stings. It all clusters into a sour blankness in his mind.

He grates his knuckles on the ancient beam in his bedroom and mutters violent dialogue from imagined confrontations with notional enemies.

Why can't you ever look at us? Look at us when we're talking to you.

The pain across his shoulders and lower neck is mad.

Ding-ding, here comes little lord mood swing.

When him and Divit spent all day watching kung fu films and German porn, doing bongs and eating strawberry laces, then went into town to meet the boys because Gemma had a free house, but all the St Eustace dickheads were in Rhymer Court trying to kick off, saw them too late, him and Divit walked straight in and started getting shit, Eustace lads, racist twats, Divit said *Ginger Minge* to a big redhead kid and then him and the kid starting slapping and chatting shit to each other and the ginger lad lobbed the P-word at Divit and Divit had his ring on and cracked the kid really sweet on the cheek, cut it open, big blob of blood on his creamy pale freckled cheek like a jam doughnut, and Shy felt a bit awkward and giddy for a second watching, buzzing scared, a lot smaller than most of these fuckers, then someone thumped him on the back of the head as he turned, then someone ran at him and walloped him in the gut, then it all went mad and he was on the ground being kicked, stunned that one punch to the stomach could wind him like this, rugby-playing psychos, kids with expensive sports kits and happy parents, bad bad situation, worrying lost, trying to cover his head, making swear-grunt noises and trying not to cry, guessing at possible outcomes, rapid-fire panic, then someone stamped hard on his ankle and that fucking hurt and he remembered learning that Rhymer Court is where they used to hang criminals in the Middle Ages and it scared him as a kid, he always walked the long way round Rhymer Court, visualised a blue-faced corpse, swinging on the rope, people passing by with their Iceland bags and buggies and Zimmer frames, and then someone kicked him in the face which didn't connect properly but scraped really sharp and surprising up over his nose and eyes like Ow ow what is this weirdo wearing Velcro trainers and that's when he cracked open furious, sprung up tangled and panting, snarling like a dog, livid off his tits tantrum scream like a toddler hurt spinning, lashing out and slashing at faces, and then he was backed up against a bench with five or six lads pissing themselves laughing saying he was about to fucking get it, *Spastic*, *what the fuck*, *he's lost it*, *calm down mentalist*, *deck him*, Divit on the ground cussing and holding his face, *Leave him alone*, thinking Bollocks do I peg it, or do I run at them like they taught us in Year 6 camp, run at the robbers in the alley screaming Waaaaaaaah, and they'll be so shocked they'll move aside, but these pricks are up so close I can smell the CK One on them, what a shitshow, was supposed to be sitting on a sofa at Gemma's getting off with Becky, maybe slipping a hand up Becky's top to rest a hand on one of her nice warm baps in her nice soft bra, she's the nicest gentlest snog, hope she's not gone off with James by the time I get there, *I know you*, said one of the St Eustace boys, *we went to Tumble Tots together, haha,* Eustace lads laughing, *What the fuck, nah, kick his fucking head in, when did you become such a gyppo, nice bomber jacket Kev, is your mum still a skank,* and Shy doesn't recognise the boy, isn't really listening, but does remember Tumble Tots, that was fun when they let us swing on the ropes across the rubber mats, he's panting like he's run a cross-country, standing there as if he's in *Tekken,* paused, ready, lost, keen to get from here to Gemma's, keen to undo the last half-hour and have Divit up off the ground, keen to stop getting himself in these situations where he wants to turn back the last half-hour, but also kind of glad to be here again, in the shit, junglist soldier – like I told ya – and he takes a glass beer bottle from the full bin beside him, smashes the neck off on the bench and swings as hard as he can at the chatty lad banging on about Tumble Tots and opens a line straight across the top of the kid's forehead, unzips the skin and watches a sheet of blood fall down like special effects, cheap and nasty, and he thinks Wow, so easy, and he thinks Oops, now I'm in proper trouble, and he sits down on the bench and covers his ears.

Just him and the field. Featureless.

Come and kill me, big ginger lad. Please turn up here one night and do me a favour.

Shy's written a brilliant thing for his English coursework about the souls of all the previous inhabitants living amongst us. An old seventeenth-century earl type, ghosts in the attic, a girl from the sixties hiding in his bedroom. It's really top-notch. And frankly pretty disturbing as well! Shy? Did you want to tell your mum about that? Come on, pal, get involved. She's driven over to talk, not to watch you sulk.

Didn't realise night in the country was so light. Undark, anti-bright. The only raver left in the field. Staying humble in the jungle.

> *You don't know yourself yet. Trust me. It's all to come. It's a multi-season job, knowing yourself. You're still in the spring.*

He's saving the music for later. The thing he always has to look forward to, which will never disappoint him. He lists as he walks. *Here Comes the Drumz. Dark Angel. Ribbon in the Sky. Gangsta Hardstep. The Burial. Mystic Stepper. Terminator II.*

Top ten.

Best of '94. Best of '95 so far.

Funeral tunes. Headphone tunes. Party tunes. Bad mood tunes. Jump up time.

Desert Island selectah.

Shy said Wait for it, wait for it, and the tune dropped and Benny shouted *BOOOOM* and hopped in circles around Shy's room and Paul hammered on the wall and shouted *Shut Up Dickheads* and Benny banged back *Fuck off, Peedy Paul* and Paul turned up his Sepultura and Shy turned up his Jumpin Jack Frost and Benny shouted *SOUNDWAAAAR* and walloped the wall and Paul shouted *I'll fucking kill you* and whacked his wall and screamed and Shy sat on his bed grinning and Amanda came running up to shut the whole thing down and docked their pool table privileges.

Jenny worming gently and expertly into his head: *Maybe you could talk about this with Iain, or your mum?*

Would that help? And does that make you feel ashamed,
Shy? Hmm? Have you made up with Calum? Do you
maybe worry what people will think, if you enjoy lessons,
if you get good marks, or is that not it?

Jenny's notebook, Jenny's pen, Jenny's posture.

And does this ghost voice sound like you? And when they
laughed and said your ideas were lame, did that upset you,
or do you not really mind what they think? Do you worry
what the others think of you, Shy? Especially Benny?

Jenny's mole on her cheek like a little choc chip,
Jenny's coffee breath, Jenny's leather sandals like a
fucking disciple of Christ.

When he went back to that girl's house and it was mmhang haha hangabout bitmore kissun and wait-a-sec-crouched in front, really like that, hahaknackerdboth of them tilting off the sloft surface off of the rworld a bit, wow that was lush, the wordl abit, happy happy K-fucked and honestly so nice, rrrsensitive a bit how hotwondering how she's titsupside down above him moving back and over his head hisdown between her legs sheet bear orbiting him peel off wet and saying hang on lemme sip a simp a glass of water gasping something good at waitand she was water or dry mouthjoke the most still with his socks onlisten to my heart she's got sofgood lot mates won't believe him, sleepsmell of chemicalspeach, fruit and powderfucked noses, throatstwinkling fairy lights listening to fuzzy instrumental hip-hop and sleeping for a bit, he sits up in bed finding his mind sharpening slightly while she sleeps and he feels grown-up and blissed out and this is such a long way from the competitive hurried tossing off and groping and fingering they've all been doing at parties at mates' houses, this is in a different time and space altogether, is he in heaven haha, she's skinning up on his tummy, she grinds her green in a plastic contraption, squeak of the lid wakes him, twists it too sticky, just give it here you hippy, hands too dry, comedown nagging, laughing at her posters, then they must've slept for a bit, then they're less wasted, feeling awake and fine, and eat some Kipling cakes and drink some Sprite and start kissing again, sugary, gentle, so far from the awkward mess of his life, and he wants to tell her all his secrets, he wants to stay here forever, sitting in her bed smoking herb, her naked top half like a miracle, naked legs intertwined warm easy, soft tickle of her pubes, telling her about his dream for a label, pinch yourself boy this is too cool, you'll never forget this, always be talking with her about how Andy C played maybe the hardest set ever, Stevie Hyper D achieving things they didn't think were possible on the mic, next-level genius, will never forget this moment, and they start shagging again, up on all fours with her holding the bed, and he looks down and watches himself going in and out, grins sleepily at Angel from *Buffy* smiling down at him, then he rests his chest on her soft warm back, one arm next to hers holding the headboard, one arm reaching down, their fingers meeting to touch as she reaches under to stroke his tired balls, then he's sat back up with a jolt with a weird shooting worry in his skull, beeeeep, hang on how come we're on the other side of the room, pulled out, bip bip bip whiiiiiiiiiiiiiine weird sheet of shame chucked over him, what, worryworry, what she's asking whatsup, hey what's up, strange panic from the base of his chest about being embarrassed or guilty and then he hits her thigh as hard as he can.

Jenny: *You did what, sorry?*

Shy: Gave her a dead leg.

Jenny: *Oh my word. Why?*

Shy: Argh. Don't know. Honestly no idea. We all give each other dead legs the whole time. Proper habit. In school, it was a thing. All the time. And for some unknown reason I just saw her leg and walloped it. I can't explain it. I was very wasted.

Jenny: *And then what happened?*

Shy: A lot of confusion, I think. Crying and shouting. I can't really remember. I was out of it. Her flatmate came in and bundled her out. I left, not sure how I got home. Never saw her again. Can't even remember her name. Not good. Not good at all. I think about it all the time. All the time.

The grass in the next field whispers.

The moon is stalking. Judging.

Breathe again. One, two, three. Up and down the hills and valleys of his chilly hands. Four, five, back again, breathe.

Amanda taught them about the Norns, the mystical Nordic sisters, sitting knitting futures, and that night Shy was woken by the weight of them sat at the foot of his bed, three ancient biddies, oddly familiar hybrids of Mum, Nana, Amanda, Thatcher, Mrs Hooper his playschool teacher, Pat Butcher, Jenny, Madge Bishop, women he's known or seen or imagined, collaged together, risen from the smudgy mess of his subconscious, staring at him, smiling, clck, clck, one of them's knitting, clck, clck, fate being looped and strung as he falls back asleep.

Knuckles turning crackling in his mind.

No, he hasn't had any more ideas about hurting himself.

No, he doesn't want to be filmed as part of the Last Chance documentary.

No, he doesn't want to buddy up with Riley on a litter pick.

No, he doesn't really think all art is gay.

No, he doesn't want his mum and stepdad to visit this Sunday.

The night is a shattered flicker-drag of these sense-jumbled memories, like he's dropped, but he's stone-cold not, he's just traipsing along, conducting memories.

Shy here has extremely disturbing dreams, but we're working on some strategies, some coping mechanisms, some night-time tricks, isn't that right, Shy?

He thinks about the tape in his Walkman and the spliff in his pocket. He's excited. Clarity. Smoke. Production values. Lift. Privacy. Control. He talks to himself, shuffles through accents: Pleasure ya can't measure, give the people what they want, squash them bubblin babies with bass, going out to all Last Chance crew in the place, all nightwalk massive, big up the backpack, sounds of the Shy One walkin, talkin, stalkin the mornin, here comes a warnin, bringin the storm in. The build, the break, the sub-quake shake. Yes mister how can I help? Anything you want, mate. Yes rudeboy, whatever you need. Jazzy, soulful, clean and spacey, some fucking nightmare metal shit, haha, whatever. Shy laughs. Ya like that do ya? Proper housey vocals, pure ragga fire. Smooth, scary, lairy. All meat no dairy. Haha. The best British invention since the steam engine? The future is here, '95 no fear.

Things are looking pretty good for you, right? Steve smiles at the whiteboard, at Shy's map of the self. Feeling good, am I right?

He can hear it, precisely, in his head, the way an Amen break washes like a wave, slots inside itself again and again, fits inside his heart, his favourite thing when it drops down to half speed, slouching, swagger, weapons close to its chest, and then it jumps up, exploding crisp and juicy, mathematical perfection, up, up and away, made by drum machines and samples but sounding like divine invention. God is a bouncy bastard who wants his people together in the dance. Rolling. Technology and soul. Hallefuckinlujah he loves the drums. Rain them down on me.

Obviously he never says any of this to Shaun, or Benny, he just says Hardcore. Nice. Yeah. Fucking love this tune.

He just grins, and nods.

He stops and looks around, suddenly aware of himself.

Carried away.

The field is staying dead still but it's tight and close around him like he's wrapped up in it. A block of night that moves with him, breathes as he breathes. Everything is pressing edge. Encroaching dense.

He doesn't want to think about what might be out here.

Posh Cal comes from the countryside and tells stories about the woods. These old hunty blokes who live in the forest and cut people up and burn them on big bonfires with all the brambles and bracken and smoky shit so nobody knows, grind the bones into pig lunch. Shiny leather high heels and kids' toys in the wood like props from ITV murder dramas, scared people running through bracken and brambles, trying to get to the safety of the big house but the big house isn't safe, it's fully stocked with violent, frustrated young male offenders, all lying awake, nightsweats in the dark Last Chance, marinating their desire to hurt people night after night in their soupy rural overlapping dreams, bad young men, blast-past-borstal bastards, lab rats, lying there while crusty ghosts from the old house crouch over them dribbling fear and violent fantasy into their ears, drip, spittle, trickle in the middle of the mean old witchy littered English woods a long way from home, a long way from any lights or cab ranks, or trust, or mums.

Haha, crack on, you fuckintwat, says Shy, and starts walking again, slight shivers in his belly.

'If the owner of the building gets planning permission to convert it into luxury self-contained flats, then Last Chance will be a thing of the past. Steve says he and his colleagues are sanguine: "Money talks, you know. But hopefully someone's inner philanthropic lion will start roaring. If not, we'll pack these kids into a caravan and take this show on the road, isn't that right, lads? *Thelma and Louise*-style last geography class, full speed into the abyss, yeah?"'

The backpack tugs with every step.

His cousin Shaun said *Just chill out a bit, mate. You're acting weird.*

Iain said *Shy likes to self-sabotage, isn't that right, cross-patch?*

Benny said he stole a Renault 5 GT Turbo, rally hatch, said he drove it into the train station ticket hall. Shy said Chinny reckon, and Benny said *Get lost, wigger, who asked you?*

Cal said *Why don't you have any armpit hair?* And Shy said Why don't you have any mates?

He threw his chair back and stormed out of a session with Jenny.

He got as far as the foot of the big staircase and he turned around, back along the corridor, and stormed in again.

Stop pretending you know me! You only know what I tell you.

OK, Shy, said Jenny.

It's not OK, said Shy.

He stands and leans forward to alleviate the pain in his back. It feels good, the weight off his shoulders, blood in his head, hands on his knees, could stay like this forever. Something that was hurting for a long time briefly not hurting.

Upside down, quiet in his head.

Admit you love the drama, Shy.

Helloooo, says the voice from his dreams. Wakey wakey, up and at 'em, Shy.

His mum and stepdad peering at him, waiting for an explanation. His stepdad asking when the Jekyll and Hyde shit will end.

His blotchy face mumbling into his crossed arms, into the kitchen tabletop, into the dark enclosure of his impatient buzzing sick-of-himself pickle, I *am* ashamed, I'm ashamed. (Leave me alone)

I don't know. I don't know.

Please pleeeeeease I'm sorry.

I wish I'd never been born.

I hate you.

I want to die.

(Boom, that'll do it . . . He feels it land, senses them flinch, like a rip in the air between them. Good.)

Fuck you both.

He treads down the old barbed-wire fence, steps over and sets off across the next field.

The stick-figure Shy walks along an arrow, left to right on top of the words: Boredom ---- Risky Behaviour ---- Hurt/Trouble ---- Shame/Guilt.

And the lighter fuel incident, Shy, do we think it fits this pattern?

I guess so, says Shy.

Yup. I think so too. I think we're getting somewhere here, says Jenny.

Urrr, if you say so, says Shy.

Something flaps out of a nearby bush with a crunkled slap. He pauses.

There are white shapes all over the field which must be stones but they could also be small white animals staying deadly still. He didn't realise the eye–brain collaboration was fucked by something as ordinary as night.

Your mum's so fat she uses a lamp post as a dildo.

Predator vs Shy. Think of a retort.

Do you think that's an appropriate wa

family apart, is that what you want? /

Some people don't have the luxury of a

go again / Don't you dare walk away /

of the hurt you've caused? / Are you tr

all this? / I am literally begging you to t

Not again,

eak to me? / Do you want to break this

believe you would choose to do this /

ium to speak to like that / Wow, here we

don't do this again / Have you any idea

destroy our lives? / What's the point of

like a human being / Come back here /

not again

This is what they make army cadets do. Go for walks with rocks on their backs. Get strong or sink. Nobody tells you to fucking *Like Yourself* in the army.

> *You're a nice boy, we live in a nice town, you've got . . . You . . . OK that's not it, hang on, OK, sorry, wait, I'm doing my best, I can do it, I'll start again.*

*Listen to me, Shy. My boy. My child. These are
drugs for pain medication, these are drugs your
nana had when she was dying, for god's sake. What
are you doing? Just answer me this, what are you
wanting to escape from? What pain are you in that
you need these? Or are you just having fun? Do
you just like getting fuzzy and lost? Are you being
pressured into this by someone? Is it Shaun?
Speak to me, I beg you.*

He doesn't want to take off the rucksack, that would
feel like breaking the rules.

If you feel like an idiot, perhaps stop behaving like one.

Amanda said she believed him about the ghost in his
room, the teenage girl in old-fashioned clothes. Amanda
doesn't judge. Sits in her dungarees with her mug of
tea and hears whatever the boys want to tell her.

Steve said he could generally do with a bit less bullshit
from Shy.

Big Owen whistled the *X-Files* theme tune.

*Whoever has stolen Shy's tapes, not funny at all, you
have until midday to put them back or the whole
school loses pool table privileges.*

The future is here and it hurts his feelings. When they said Last Chance might be closing he felt everything tighten and sour inside himself. He stomped about looking for trouble, he barged and argued, he started a fight in the TV room. Shoved and spitty-snarled and tried to scrape Jamie's face and everyone laughed and chanted *Schizo Shy* and Steve held him back, arms like a trap, shushing him like a baby.

See? Even nice lads like Shy lose the plot.

His well-used copy of *Men's World* lies flat beneath his mattress. The middle pages, Jo Guest in white underwear, are imprinted on his mind. A second-hand jazz mag looked at a thousand times. Seen better days, those pages. He should have given it to Posh Cal. Whittle your dick off.

Any warning signs, Shy, notice them and recognise them for what they are. Be aware of what you're feeling, and how it's affecting what you're doing. You're the driver of this vehicle, yes?

I'm a junglist, baby, don't try to change me.

When he was a boy he looked to me, a child to a mother, you know, he faced me, for his food and his comfort, his safety and his . . . everything. I was his world, or at least the central part of it. We were facing each other. And then he turned away, as people do. Perhaps boys, especially. Maybe that's normal. Perhaps he'll turn back.

Shy? says Jenny. What do you think about that?

He wonders if his shoulders will have the red underskin bruise from the straps. The kind of thing they mention in a post-mortem scene.

Ah, very clever, you've written 'I can't be bothered' for every question. This is really tiresome, Shy. Look here: magnetism. You liked magnetism when we did it. What point are you trying to prove, trashing the paper?

Benny explains to the group what it was like in the town he grew up in, getting pulled over for no reason, getting searched, opening his mouth and being told to stop getting aggro. It's not an excuse for what he did, he says, but part of his story. Racist teachers, racist po-po. From the relative safety of Last Chance, he can see how things worked.

They're all getting better at telling their stories.

Shy says he understands.

Benny says *No. That's my point. You totally don't.*

> Flesh under his fingernails turned out to be his own,
> from the gouges on his thighs. Contusions on both
> shoulders suggest a very heavy load.
>
> Scarring on his arms dates back a year or two.
>
> Can't see any signs of a struggle.
>
> *If this triangle is you, Shy, here in the middle, living*
> *here with the others, with me, with Amanda, with*
> *the staff, who's outside? Draw them on the map.*

His mum and stepdad. His dead nan, his nice aunt
Trish, his cousin Shaun, Gill and Michael, his mates
Divit and Nathan, some boys from school, and then
Brockie, Ray Keith, Grooverider, Shy FX, Dr S. Gachét,
Andy C, Mickey Finn, he keeps writing names on the
board and then he starts on MCs, Det, GQ, Skibadee,
and Steve is laughing, *Go for it, Shy, this is your map,*
this is your world. You forgot Randall, too hot to handle!

Shy grins, embarrassed, and mock-shoots Steve with
a two-finger gun.

Adults tease him better, almost a form of kindness. The boys just rip and rip at each other, endless patterns of attack and response, like flirting's grim twin.

Shy's balls haven't dropped
Riley's mum is a prozzie
Ash has only got seven pubes
Shy needs a fake ID to buy fags
Benny and Jenny in a tree
Posh Cal got a rib removed so he can blow himself
Paul sucks dick
Cal and Shy are bumboys
Jamie wants to root Amunda

Vicious tricks and little overlays of owed favours, perceived slights and simmering fault lines of beef and threat. You can't trust anyone. That's why he loves the music so much. It promises, and it delivers. He's secure in the sound. Alone in his headphones. No barrier, no game. It welcomes him in.

Gentlemen, you stink. Let's wash more and fight less.

He stayed up late in the TV room talking with Posh Cal about girls. He told him about the girl on the campsite in Wales, how they did it unprotected, how he came before he was properly in, how he walked with her three miles into town for the morning-after pill.

59

He's got to cross the ploughed field and it's oddly hard work, bumpy mud sticking to his shoes, flints erupting glinting in the moonlight. From the top windows of the house this field looks flat but these are knee-high ridges of crumbling ground. Heavy work. Trippy. It's hard on the eyes. He's feeling a bit sorry for himself now.

Cal said *Oh man, I've been there, it's like climbing a tree and falling straight off the first branch.*

The next day Cal walked straight into the dining room and told everyone about *One-pump Shy.*

Piaow-piaow, Jamie sang. *Watch out, slags, it's Shy Montana with his cream machine.*

Why no owls, he wonders. Why no twit-twoos in the dark woods behind the house? No breeze. He's heading into bluey still nothingness. Everything seems behind him, in a clump. A fug. Last Chance and before that, slowed down, sped up, seems years since he moved here, seems like yesterday he left primary school and went back one year later and laughed at how small and low the urinals were. He felt so big and grown-up leaving primary. Little muppet. Time's been the least reliable fucker these last few years. He locks horns with the hours of the day, with what's happening just behind him, with the big hot pressure of next. Time is something to get wasted and escape from. Bullied by time. Lied to, hemmed in and taunted. Best to pass out and wake up further down the line.

> The end of the world, not getting a coach to Milton Keynes to go dancing and take Es with his friends, that's what set him off. Imagine. No resilience. Spoilt apocalypse all day every day.

Hard work, getting harder, hacking through voices. His eyes are buzzing from trying to work out the depth and shape of things in the weirdly light night. He pities himself, trudging along the muddy blind path, caught up in himself. This is why people wear boots. His Classics are ruined.

> You are a stupid lucky bastard, Shy. You are a lucky, lucky little bastard. Pretending you're hard. Look at your crash net. A mum who loves you. A good stepdad. Food. Care. This place. Me. Amanda. Owen. Not prison. You had all these chances. Eh? Wasn't so easy for the others, was it? You've seen how this country works. Police, judges. Walk a mile in Benny's shoes. Yeah? Don't take the piss, alright? Hello? Earth to Shy? Don't pretend you can't hear me.

Smells like the damp mat in the back of his nan's car, like underneath a log, the back corner of the garage where his toy fort rotted one summer to the next. Wet wood.

> *You have to take it on trust, until we design a time machine. Listen. You won't be defined by who you are now, by 1995-Shy. You won't even much remember him. 2005-Shy will look back on this and agree with me. He'll be like, I was just around the corner, Shy. Just get past this bit. He'll say, Steve was right!*

Umm, sorry I threatened to kill my stepdad.

Sorry I got expelled.

Sorry I sold those kids a bit of dry mud wrapped in cling film.

Not especially sorry about any of these things, to be honest.

OK.

Alright. Easy. Here goes.

Sorry I keyed my mum's car. Genuinely. That's a real one. It was a bullshit thing to do and I regret it.

Sorry I sometimes lose control of, like, everything.

Sorry I bottled that ginger lad, obviously.

Sorry I nicked that Doc Scott record, haha not sorry at all.

Sorry I sprayed *PUNANI* on Liam's wall, but it was fucking class. Not sorry about that.

Sorry I lost Kelly's bag of MDMA.

Alright, here's one. Sorry I acted like a twat at Nana's funeral. That nags at me. I feel bad about that.

There's a lot, I guess. Sorry Becky, sorry Gill and Michael, sorry Mum, sorry Iain.

> *The Disappointment Gap again, Shy. Remember? We thought your Sleep Cave would help, and it didn't, so you're anxious and cross with yourself. This is a Loss-Focused thinking style, right? Remember?*
>
> *Shy?*
>
> *Shy? Are we listening?*
>
> *OK, headphones off, please, Shy, that's just rude.*
>
> *I think this music isn't helping, so fast and choppy and metallic. If we're looking for reasons why you're not getting REM sleep, we might look no further than the Walkman, right? It's very ON, and we need you OFF.*

Shy? Anyone home? I really did hope we were getting past this sort of behaviour.

He wants to write to the boy whose face he cut open and say something.

He wants some back-and-forth with him, rather than the framed event so big and unarguable in everyone's minds. He can't really hold any thoughts or feelings steady in his head about having done the thing, so he wonders if the lad has any clarity about having had it done to him. He wonders about the scar.

Carrying a heavy bag of sorry.

Strange clouds lit neon-blue by the moon, bumpled like an acne cheek. Fleshy. The solid world dissolves then coheres, like broken sleep, and he shambles into it, remembering.

> *You mustn't do that to yourself, Shy. My little baby. You mustn't hurt yourself like that. You've only got one body.*

Jenny says *Like Iain? How so?*

Shy says Cleaning his car. Playing golf. Lying awake worrying about his gutters.

Jenny says *Oh, come on. What if he likes his car? What if he likes golf? Does everyone have to enjoy the same things you do? That wouldn't work, would it?*

Shy says Hmff.

Jenny says *I'd say there's bigger worries in this world than turning into Iain.*

He snorts and spits and hoicks the backpack up higher on his painful shoulders.

The other teaching staff and I feel you're taking up more than your fair share of space at the moment. A lot of our attention. Just dial things down a bit, please.

[The camera noses into the TV room, three huge sunken brown sofas, a mini basketball hoop on the back of the door, the pool table, piles of *Mixmag* and *Loaded* and *FHM*. Lounging boys in smelly trainers, restless and goading.]

'We try and incentivise good behaviour, says Steve, rather than punish bad, but there are limits. Very funny, guys. That'll do, I think. Sorry, some showing-off going on here. Yes, very good, Shy, your fifteen minutes of fame. There are new pool cues arriving today, so the boys are a smidge overexcited. Sorry.'

Jenny says *Can you give me an example?*

Shy says Like, like getting obsessed and frustrated about tiny random things and then being ashamed and embarrassed that little things get so big in my head. Or massive shit beyond my control.

Jenny says *OK, and can you give me an example of some massive shit?*

Shy says Ummm. Sorry, I'm just really tired today.

Jenny says *Take your time.*

Shy says OK. The Amazon rainforest being chopped down and people slagging off Sting for giving a fuck like they've ever done anything whereas Sting's working his arse off.

Jenny says *Really?*

Shy says It winds me up.

He stops and looks about. He feels very alone, very small, very ignorant. Humbled by a thick sudden worry. He needs to crack on. Don't let the overthinking strangle in. Little ideas left to grow unmanageable in the massive gabber hangar of his night terrors. *Worries in the dance.* Huge sound system mashing out any other noise. Paranoid and thirsty. Don't go night-raving with a backpack of flints.

> *I'm not saying this to make you feel guilty, but have you ever thought of your mum as a human being, outside you? Did you know that the lake of depression you've been describing falling into is a lake your mum knows well? She's been climbing out of that lake and now she's seeing her son run tumbling in. Is anything I'm saying interesting you at all, Shy?*

When his mum said she had gone and bought a ten-pack of Number Ones and he could have those cigarettes and he could even smoke those cigarettes at home, in the driveway, so long as he put the butts in the wheelie bin, on the condition that he sit down and watch a holiday vid with her and Iain, and he agreed so she gave him the fags and he went out and smoked one, came in and joined them in the living room and Iain had his camcorder box down from the loft and the VHS tapes labelled all neat in their cases and he popped in *WATER SPRINKLER / CHARMOUTH '86* and they watched the video and Little Shy went pegging it off into the sea and his mum laughed and Iain laughed and Shy hopped and skipped in the shallows and pegged it back and then he tap-tap-tapped at a rock with his special hammer but didn't find a fossil, then Iain flew a kite while his mum laughed at him, then his mum ran down to the sea, squealed at the cold and ran back laughing, shouting *Turn it off, Iain, turn it off, you bugger*, then Iain did a commentary on Shy lifting stones, *Surely not, surely the young lad's not going to get a boulder of that size up and off the OOH CRIKEY MIKEY HE'S GONE AND DONE IT, bend your knees, mate, unbelievable scenes here at the World's Strongest Boy competition*, and then it cuts to the back garden later that summer and Shy is in his Spidey suit, too small, short on his skinny wrists and ankles, wet and clinging to him, leaping through the sprinkler, and as he reaches Iain he star-jumps and shouts *BORN* into the camcorder lens and as he runs away he sings *in the USA*, and turns at the end of the garden by the greenhouse and comes back again, leaping through the sprinkler, *BORN*, sprinting back up the garden, *in the USA*, again and again, and Iain is chuckling and you can hear Gill and Michael and his mum in the background chatting and laughing, and the tape ends and his mum says *See, that wasn't so hard* and Shy says Don't fucking bother, Mum, and Iain says *Hey, hang on a minute,* and Shy says You can get lost, Iain, and Iain says *Woah there,* and Shy imitates him, Woah there, and kicks the box of tapes across the living room floor and leaves, into the hallway and slamming the door to the overlapping sounds of *Here we go again* and *We can't win* and *Come back here this second* and *Let him go,* and he has the song stuck in his head as he skulks around the park smoking and spitting and feeling boring but that's all he knows, just that bit, he doesn't know the rest of the song.

Is it true you boned a farmer's daughter, ooo-arrrrr,
Shy, Shy, oi don't fucking walk away from me, batty
boy, did you fuck a few cows too, you manky little
bastard. Oi Shy, don't go, we're just having a laugh.
Shy?

After the one-pump thing he went to the pigeonholes and stole Cal's post. He opened it to check for cash because Cal's a rich little bitch, then he buried it deep in the bin.

Little things. A few times. Lick his wounds, lash back out.

He talked earnestly in class about everything that's good in UK music coming from black culture, and Jamie said *Awww bless, when he grows up Shy wants to be black,* so he stuffed Jamie's Ellesse hoodie down the back of the airing cupboard tank.

'There is no wealth but life', mate. Start by getting
up, maybe have a wash, maybe consider a clean
pair of boxers, then get dressed, and let's see where
today takes us, eh?

He took a gulp of his bedside water last week and it was still-warm piss, frothy, and he retched and punched his pillow, tried not to cry, boarded up, locked in a haunted house with other boys like him. He cannot win.

What I will say is that you give as good as you get,
Shy, and if you dish it out you've got to take it.
Maybe try keeping yourself to yourself for a bit, eh?

Visions, night terrors, voices, conversations on the phone with his mum about his psychic great-granny, conversations with Steve about William Blake and migraines and ayahuasca, conversations with the doctor about pills and avoiding weed and horror films, conversations with Jenny about fight and flight, fresh air and exercise, recognising the itch behind his eyes, tired lines of thought, repetitions, uncanny hunches, it's like, he's trying to describe it, it's like, like a roll of barbed wire scrunched inside me, scraping underneath, all day every day, and then it gives way to something slippy, busy, sometimes I feel really excited and bouncy and other people's thoughts are all buzzing in my whole body like I can tell what they're feeling, easy pictures, clear sequences, like I know exactly what's going on before and after, like my brain has found its groove, then it's gone again. Just sludge.

Shit. Just me again.

The mind is a universe, black holes and all, says Steve.
It's mad, and that's a fact.

He wouldn't be sinking so deep with every step if he
wasn't carrying a rucksack of flints, *and that's a fact.*

He smiles.

Cal felt guilty about the one-pump thing and made it
up to Shy with a ten-bag of skunk for his birthday, the
very last of which he has saved, and is about to smoke.

What the fuck, Shy's got the voice of an angel! Oi Shy,
Shy, sing that again, listen up, check out jungle-bunny's
singing.

Benny shaved Shy's head, grade 2 all over, and Jamie
said Shy looked like a dying orphan in a charity advert
and Benny said *Oi Jamie, howbout you fuck off for a*
change.

The local MP visited the Last Chance for a walk-
around, press the flesh, a photograph or two, a little
bit of architectural history. Yellow corduroys, holding
his breath in the TV room, wiping his hand after every
shake, talking about *Education is salvation, my young*
friends, and *Any questions, anyone?* Steve saying *Boys,*

come on, you're not usually lost for words and Shy polite-
ly raising his hand and asking:

I wondered, sir, is it part of the training for, like, becoming an MP, or have you always been such a cunt?

Booyaka, Shy.

His chest buzzes warmly remembering it, the nerve,
the timing, the reaction.

Fair play, Selecta.

They'd argued about the MP in class. Nice Andy the
Bearded History Teacher had said it was good that
they were riled up, but what next? How are they going
to make a fairer society? With what tools and ideas?
Just anger?

*Some of you will vote in the '97 election, that's a powerful
weapon.*

Jamie said *A sawn-off shotgun's a powerful weapon.*

Shy was angry with Nice Andy the Bearded History
Teacher last week and he can't remember why. Boun-
cing round Last Chance like a pissy little pinball.

*God, this little gang here and their music. Endlessly
theorising about it. Always about how bad*

something is. How hard. That's it, isn't it, Shy?
Shy here's the governor-general of drum n bass,
converting them all. It's really his thing. He has these
highly coveted plastic packs of tapes and he loans
them out to the lads.

Hard. Dark. Lethal. Renegade. Brutal. That's what
they want, apparently. All huddled together,
nodding, one headphone each. I've embarrassed
them now, look.

When he was about fifteen his mum mentioned that
she'd given his old box of Hot Wheels to the church
playgroup and it sent him over the edge. He called her
a mean bitch, and she flinched and her face unspooled
to frightened and she was shaking, pacing the kitchen, holding her hands like a praying nun, she just
couldn't understand, she didn't know why he'd want
those old toys, he hadn't looked at them in years, and
she couldn't believe he'd speak that way to his mother,
she was just trying to do a clear-out, she didn't think
he liked his old cars anymore, hadn't seen him play
with Hot Wheels in years, and Shy screamed Shut up
and Shut up and Shut up, Mum, and he banged his
forehead on the table again and again and his mum
was saying *Stop it, darling, I beg you* and he hated her
and wanted to tunnel down into the earth and die
and his mum was saying *Talk to me, please explain* and

he covered his ears and hummed furious serrated basslines into his red closed mind like an electrical storm for as long as it took and when he looked up she was gone and his vision was skittering black worms and he couldn't remember why he was so angry.

And this happened again and again.

Shy wonders why.

When he woke up twice in his nightmare last week he'd gone down to the pond and walked in over his head, eyes open, but every time he tried to lie down, the second his weight was on the bottom of the pond, someone would reach in and yank him out, lift him by his hair, hoicked up gasping to the top, which is the attic bathroom, under the surface calm, ripped up, pulled hair, back to the bathroom, graffiti on the beam, under the surface alarm, metal pipe running right through him, a naked woman half-Amanda half-stranger pegging it round and round the pond, faster than a human can run, like a sped-up video, bathroom, back under, making a noise like the foxes shagging at night, barbed dicks howling, whoosh up out of the pond, back in the bathroom, carved beam laughing, just as he manages to lie down on the soft mattress of the bottom of the pond, whoosh, sucked back up, hair being yanked out of his head, back in the bathroom, half-Amanda screeching and wheeling around the pond like she's on rails, like the trains on a tight track at the steam fair, the ghost girl's face on Amanda's body, slapping around and around the lap of the pond, white flash, young girl running, metal bar in Shy's tummy, up his back, into his mouth, if he falls it'll smash his throat, shunt up into his skull, so the only way out is the big old porcelain sink, knock himself dead, clock himself out, shock himself or stop himself seeing the looping naked milk-him hair-pulled hair-pain hard-on iron bar in the middle of the pond, that'll do it, anything, smash himself into shutdown, that'll do it, any way out of the dream, out of the hole, and he lines himself up, here goes, quick and clean, cool way to go, smiling teeth bared grinning in the mirror which is the pond which is round and round and a flat round sorry, doesn't recognise himself in the chundering thunderstorm of again and again still Shy still hearing, still thinking, and he slams his face down on the sink as hard as he can, smash expecting shattered bone-sharp cold oblivion but the sink is a cotton-soft pillow smelling of him and he wakes up gasping in his bedroom, RAM Records poster, scalp burning, heart two-step shat-parping in his chest, blam, blam, clack/clack, fucking hell what was that, blam, blam, clack/clack slap the wall next to his bed, heart attack, can't handle this, worth dying just to not have these dreams anymore, it's this stupid haunted house, every room like a well-stocked video store of people who lived and died and had appalling dreams in this house, panting, Shy's short breaths like the pitter-patter of footsteps jogging laps, and then the duvet lifts up at his feet and he screams but no sound comes out and in his dream he is livid to be tricked into thinking he'd woken, double level, screams but his throat is padded hopeless, someone else panting, the sound of someone panting, the duvet is lifted off him just like his mum used to do on a hot night to cool him, to waft him, but it's Benny, several Benny faces chocking on him and on him and on him again like fever repeat VHS stuck or a scratch on the vinyl and the soft twist of duvet dives in and starts kissing Shy, licking Shy, pressing Shy down, and it's rough and weird and toughly good, reaching down, tugging him in, and Amanda is a young girl in Benny's body, pressing down on Shy's shoulders so he can't move, Benny is biting Shy's lips, then his nose, pulling at Shy's hair, won't let you drown broseph, won't fucking let you, yank up hairline, tight in the twist, Amanda's got Benny's face but smells of carpet and they're wanking Shy, multiple arms, they taste a bit metallic, cosy river, rust BO and inside salt-warm like a fanny, and he's trying to say stop but his head is under the water so it's just bubbles and Benny's saying *Get ready*, doesn't want to come, mustn't wet the bed, *Shy get ready*, and the round-the-pond loop is attached to his stomach, lurch like he's going to shit, like he's going to come, and a whole crowd of people jostle him undone and shove him around and around towards the security fence and he's struggling to breathe, too wasted, but people are screaming and whistling for the drop and Benny says *Here goes, here goes, ready, here goes, this is my favourite tune*, too wasted so he lifts the sink up and boom, bassline smashes down onto Shy's face and Shy wakes up bright white clear and alert, with an echo-image of his teeth and jaws splashed red and hammer-horror fake onto the rim of the sink, now he's awake, Jesus Christ, now he's awake, RAM Records poster, scalp burning, heart two-step shat-parping in his chest, boom/blap boom/blap, clackety-clackety, heart attack, damn man, I'd rather die than be this fucked night after night by these dreams, and then the duvet lifts up and Shy starts screaming and Shy's mum is trying to cool him down, Steve is in the room trying to wake Shy up, Benny is swearing and pacing, the girl in old-fashioned clothes saying *Let us wake up, leave us alone, give him a second*, Shy's mum is still in the dream saying *Ready, waft, ready, waft, is that better*, and the cool duvet is better, she knows what to do when Shy has a night terror, just sort his duvet out, he's all caught up, mate you've woken the whole house up, make sure he's awake, he doesn't like getting trapped between asleep and awake, he never has, poor lamb.

*I'm going to advise you to find some middle ground,
Shy. You're very up when you're up, and ever so
down when you're down. It's bloody exhausting, if
I'm honest.*

He's almost there and he's hungry and his back hurts.

*Shy's a ghost, innit. That's why he's so white. Shy
died twenty years ago, now he's haunting us.*

Nice Andy the Bearded History Teacher: *I want to talk
to you about this properly, with the others, not crouched on
the floor of the toilets crying. Alright?*

Shy: Sure.

Nice Andy the Bearded History Teacher: *There's other
options, mate. Come on, hop up.*

Shy: Just genna splash my face, I'll be two secs.

Nice Andy the Bearded History Teacher: *Alright. See
you in a minute.*

Shy: Alright.

Nice Andy the Bearded History Teacher: *Okey doke.*

Shy: Cheers.

Nice Andy the Bearded History Teacher: *No worries.*

Shy: I'm really sorry I can't stop crying, Andy.

Nice Andy the Bearded History Teacher: *Come here, giz a hug.*

I said to him, there'll be rapists, violent offenders, not murderers I don't think, but some very disturbed young men, and he stood up, came round the table and said, Mum, I'm a very disturbed young man, *and I said, No poppet, you're lost, that's different, and he said,* Mum, listen to me, I know you love me, but it's not different. I'm not lost. I'm right where I got myself, *and I said Oh, darling, no, and he said,* Mum, shh. Whatever. A new school. My last chance. I'm going to take it.

There's more to life than drum n bass. There's more to life than getting wasted.

He walks across the gravel track to the picnic table, four neat cereal-crunch footstep sounds.

You're taking up too much space.

And there it is.

Deceptive, inky-smooth, silent, at ease with its unknown weight.

The pond.

Duck shit. Pigeon shit. Thistle. Diesel. Scrawny ash.
Nettles. Veteran oak with red 'risk' mark. Struggling
willow. Old rope. Plastic six-pack ring. Hard dry dog
shit in a black plastic bag. Duckweed. Empty blue
Rizla packet. Barn owl pellet. Wet wipe. Buddleia.
Rat-tail plantain. Safeway bag. Foster's can. Cigarette
butt. Meadowsweet. But all Shy sees is the night
reflected sharper than the real thing, crisp on the flat
black slab of the pond.

He sits on the picnic table with his feet on the bench.

He puts his headphones on and presses play.

Hidden in his hood in a perfect world of breaks and
basslines and rapid-fire patter. Lifted off.

He leans back to let the table take the weight of the
rucksack. He groans in relief.

The moon is behind a cloud. It's a different density of
night by the pond.

He stretches a leg out, takes the fag packet from his
pocket, removes the joint, crumples the pack and
throws it on the ground. He strokes the well-built
spliff between two fingers, smoothing the cone. He
bites off and spits the twisted end, then he lights it up.

He enjoys it so, so much. He gargles it thickly, tasting,

lets it trickle up from his mouth slow and snakey into his nose, then he blows rings, then he takes great big deep tugs and pouts and soft-brrrrrrs lung-sized clouds into the milky night and then he holds the joint in front of him in his fingertips, friendly lighthouse cherry at heart height, and he says truthfully: I love you, but he can't hear his own voice because the tunes are so loud in his ears. *Inside the ride*. If he had a horn he'd blast it. *Express how you're feelin*. He usually wishes the MC was a bit less chatty and repetitive on this mix but tonight he's glad of the company. *Yup yup yup in the town, up in the town, dance right now and move around*. He thumbs his clipper and holds it up, smiling. *Trust me, trust me, run that*.

Nodding and swaying. He dips his neck and bobs and looks to the left, surveys the pond, and looks to the right, nods at the night, warm in his heart, mind all bright. He puts his hands inside his hood and presses the headphones hard against his ears, then he opens his arms out wide and looks up at the sky, then he bops and dips double time, then he hunches over so his head is almost in his lap and the backpack is lifted off the table, then he juts his head left right left right like he's watching tennis at 170 bpm. Then he sits up and stabs at the air with his spliff, then he makes little gun fingers with both hands and points again and again at the ground in front of him, then he nods his head at half the speed and rolls his shoulders around, then he waves his right hand in the air whipping circles, then he leans back on the bag of stones and grins.

He holds his lighter up.

Lighterrrrrrr.

He finishes the joint. Closes his eyes for the last hot treacly resin burn of the roach on his lip. Best bit. Then he pinches it, sits up and flicks it.

He steps down off the bench and grimaces at the sky. He smiles and says Yes, mate.

The weight surprises him again and he almost falls backwards onto the bench. Wobbles and laughs. The pain across his shoulders is intense but he's blissed out, headrushed and beaming. He steps on the spot in time to the music but can only manage a few seconds. Even a half-arsed trudge is hard graft; the flints are weighing him down.

He puts his hood down and takes off his headphones.

He presses stop.

The world is atrociously bare and quiet.

Cold ears.

He wraps the headphone cord a few times around
the Walkman, tight to keep the little tape door shut.
He kisses the Walkman and says Original Junglist
Massive. He puts it on the picnic table, pats it twice
and says: Thank you.

He turns to look up in the direction of the house and
hears a rustle straight in front of him, a dragging
shuffle sound of dry leaves or feet being moved, but
all he can see is the track, the hedge, the bottom field.
Biggish animal, or cautious human. There could
be someone in that hedge, or behind, hiding in the
field watching him. He might have walked right
past someone lying on the ploughed ground, a dark
shape disguised against a dark field or crouched in the
shadow of the hedge, or hiding behind a tree. Someone
out here up to some unhealthy night-time business,
some country nutbar behaving strangely. He turns
and looks at the pond and the feeling fades. It's only a
worry when he looks back, so he gets up and wanders
onwards, past wondering.

He mumbles a bassline to himself as he walks towards
the edge of the pond and feels a flickering temptation
to rewind, backwards squeal up the field to bed, to
dreams, to Steve and Amanda and the boys, to revision
and breakfast baps on Saturdays and making mixtapes
and his pillow, his duvet, his . . . His feet are in.

> *bom bom bobbabom-bobbabom*
> *bom bom bobbabom-bobbabom*

Wow.

Cold water.

Jesus.

Very stoned.

He is off the wire-clad plank and into the gunky
shallows, firm underfoot but slippy, and his trainers
and socks are straight away wet through as he shuffles
forward. The ground is a bit softer as he gets in up
to his knees. His ripples move calmly out. Nothing is
quacking or flapping. The pond is asleep. It's squelchy
now. His jeans are heavy. It's not as cold as he thought
it would be, but it's pretty fucking chilly.

Little trickles and lapping drip-plop sounds from the
wading body in the water.

Up to his waist.

The weeds or whatever they are on the bottom of the pond are tangling his feet so he takes higher steps and sloshes forward, dragging his hands alongside him, remembering how cold the water was at Durdle Door. Last in. Last Chance lads on a summer excursion, behaving well or they're back in the bus. No smoking, no tombstoning, no frightening the locals. He couldn't bring himself to get in past his waistline and everyone was shouting and laughing at his tippy-toeing, at his skinny body and ultra-pale skin. *Shy's got the body of a dead man. Shy is so white he glows!* Laughing and gasping, getting dragged and dunked. Happy day. They stayed in so long their fingers were wrinkled. Shy's shoulders had handprint smears where he'd done his own sun cream.

It's not getting any deeper in the pond. Liquid rustling, slip trickling, step by step, everything blueblack, oily and sharp, moon back, slow tangled mesh in his thoughts. The reflection of the trees on the water is the neatest thing he's ever seen. Nobody told him night outside a town was like this. Flat to a fault but focused. Snuffling quiet. They should tell kids stuff like this. Tell them night's like outer space.

He's almost in the middle of the pond, by the little duck island. He sees the circle of his own intrusion, quietly widening.

Stoned repetitions pester his brain and the pond smells of cum's muddy cousin. Goose shit and metal and farmyard fust.

He turns to face the picnic table, the house, the life. He sighs and kneels down. Nice and soft. Shoulders, neck and head above the surface. Ripples calmly back away from him.

He leans forward and puts his chin in the water, looking across the smooth skin of the pond. He keeps his lips tightly closed. His heart is beating so fast and then just as he's closing his eyes, he sees them.

Over by the reeds.

He keeps his eyes shut for a second and the shape of them is printed, negative, inexplicable. At the invisible point between the world he understands and the one he doesn't, on the horizon of the pond.

Two shapes.

He opens his eyes and straightens back up. Ripples disturb the surface.

Ow. Rucksack. Everything is waterlogged.

Just along from the planked section where he entered the pond, on the other side of the big spiky bushes of grass and rushes. Two . . . things.

He stays still and watches for a while, waiting for them to move, waiting for his brain to offer some ideas, anything at all, as to what the fuck they are.

His breathing's loud. He waits. Whatever they are, they aren't moving.

Then they do move, slightly.

They're floating, he thinks. Are they . . . What's the word? The pink plastic things for boats.

Rrrrr, come on.

Buoys. Are they buoys?

They can't be, they're not round enough. They're uneven. It's hard to tell how big they are but they're probably as big as Shy's rucksack, a bit bigger. The moonlight mucks about with scale and depth.

He stands up painfully heavy, slooshing through the water uncertainly, peering. He wants to see. They don't seem alive, because they're not responding to him. They seem solid, plastic or metal, but they don't look like they're fixed or anchored in any way. Maybe some kind of floating duck house or fish-feeding gizmos. But they're not identical; one is smaller, flatter. They're glossy in the moonlight, like they have a sheen, or a cling film cover. Eugh. He hates cling film.

Fuck's sake, he says, and starts gently wading towards them, away from the middle of the pond.

Knowing this weird tractory shithole, they're probably some kind of farming gadget, a feeding tool or temperature checker, like those robo-helmets stuck up in the trees behind the house. Maybe they're cleaning the pond, slow-releasing some kind of natural cleaner, or hoovering up the slime. Something scientific.

Jeezy Creezy, it boggles the mind how little I know about stuff, thinks Shy, almost cheerfully. Steve would know. Steve knows so much about all sorts of shit. He gathers up facts like he's stockpiling.

Am I being stupid, he wonders. Am I just baked and confused? The closer he gets, the less able he is to see what they are. They're *un*-clarifying themselves as he approaches.

He slips on the slimy bottom and almost falls.

This FUCKINRUCKSACK.

He stops, waiting to see if they move. He doesn't want to get electrocuted or set off some kind of alarm. If it was the daytime he feels sure he wouldn't be creeping over ready to shit his pants in the almost physical pain of not knowing what he's looking at. Blame the night, taking the dimensions out of everything. He can imagine a comic moment with a sad wet audience of one when he gets over, sees what they are, feels silly, feels tricked by the night, haha, what a plonker. Like a Magic Eye poster, he just needs his brain and his eyes to work together, help him out.

He has a wee. It feels good. A momentary hot-water-bottle warmth, then gone.

He's three or four metres away when he begins to feel with dread-certainty that they are animal. They are some kind of bloated, perhaps inflated, dead thing. Hopefully dead. But if they were dead they would smell, wouldn't they? Dead things stink, especially dead wet wild things. So they're probably models. Casts. Maybe not real. Funfair animals with all the paint cracked off. Dumped in the pond.

He backhand shoves a wave, not much more than a ripple by the time it reaches them, but enough to make them bob slightly against the reeds. Yup. They're dead.

His mind shuffles through animals. Pigs, dogs, foxes, sheep. Mini fat goats? Fuck's sake. How big is a stoat? Chubby baby deer? Otters? They're almost round, little arms, little back legs, a sort of snout. Boars? Like in *Asterix*? Are they models of boars, maybe hunters use them to shoot at? His body is hurting so much now, it's like he's been whacked on the back with a baseball bat.

He turns and squishily wades back to the plank, emerging from the shallows like a skinny Godzilla, up and out of the pond, baggy squelching. He wriggles his arms out from the straps and drops the backpack which cracks to the ground and WHOOSH, he is weightless, like the door frame party trick, or an anti-gravity stunt, he is a space-stepping ket-cadet, giggling, wow, so bouncy, it feels great, so light, so nice to be able to move, bend, stretch. He walks over feathery-light in the legs and grabs one of the reedy bulrushy things. Like a Philly Blunt on a stick. It'll do for a poker. But when he holds it out it flops and bends. He chucks it and goes to the forlorn-looking willow tree and selects a long thin branch. It's hard to snap. He has to rip and twist and peel and yank and the tree is making a fuss, trying to piss him off, then he gets it off and strips away some of the smaller twigs.

He remembers the rustling in the hedge.

He stays still and listens.

Nothing. Nobody. Just him dicking about on the shadowy blue stage of his stupid drama.

He takes his willow stick and wades back into the cold dirty water, and as he comes around the reed clump he sees them, curved and quiet, huddled together like giant capsized rubber toys in a dirty bath.

On their backs.

He imagines a gigantic toddler, thirty foot tall, creeping out here in the bedtime night and taking a shallow bath, driving his little plastic toys around the pond, *brrrrrooooom, nee-naw, nee-naw, sploosh, kapow*, and a disembodied voice from above telling him to wash, to remember to scrub his armpits, his bum, and the toddler staying very, very still, because he can hear someone coming.

Shy slides through the water, getting closer and closer.

These things were clearly once hairy, but the hair has rotted away or rubbed off and is only visible in patches now. They have a leathery surface which is glossy on the sides where they're wet, matt on the top like an old handbag. They have little trotters, so again he thinks maybe they're pigs. Maybe an abattoir has illegally dumped two unwanted corpses. Both their heads are facing away. He wishes he had a torch. Not-quite-seeing is maddening. His eyes are so fucking tired.

Why don't they smell?

He reaches with his stick and gives the larger one a poke. He flinches. His body is rigid in fright, ready to judder or recoil. His stick makes a Tupperware *thuck* sound. It can't be an animal with a hard case, can it? Could it be really old, like, mummified? Bog beasts? He knows about peat. Are there any peat bogs near here? Could they have been belched up from under the pond where they've been encased in mud for a thousand years? Is this a totally stupid idea? Amanda said there's mad-rich people round here who keep exotic animals, maybe that's it, maybe this is a pair of rare display hogs, imported, chucked in the pond and rotting. Maybe they misbehaved and the owners let them escape, but they couldn't hack the climate, the rain, the lack of things to hunt.

The larger one, the one he poked, floats slowly round, revealing its face.

Fuck *off*, no no no, Shy whispers, as it turns into view and the moon lights up a little set of white fangs, a dry-fixed snarl, vicious with a hint of bliss.

He squirms and backs off a bit. It's got to be some kind of racoon or otter, leathery and taut, some kind of extinct giant vole or whatever the hell lived in ponds or swamps in the deep old days. He can see what must have been the original shape of its head beneath the swollen meaty ridges around the teeth, two stripes of darker hair just visible, pale on the sides. It's ringing some kind of Natural History Museum punishment bell, one of the first times he got in real trouble, climbing over the barrier, mounting an okapi, his teacher screaming *Get off, get DOWN THIS INSTANT*, hoping his classmates would think he was cool, knowing it would be a shallow buzz even if they did, hoping too late he wouldn't break the okapi, he can remember the feeling of the animal's back, strong but hollow, soft one way, scratchy thick the other, nothing remotely to do with life, a totally dead encounter, but that's not what's happening here, time or water or sunshine or torture have done something else to these Unidentified Floating Objects, it's like they've paused at the exact midpoint between living things and decomposed things, when not even God could tell them if they were alive or dead, perhaps they can't even tell each other, but they try, they stay close, just in case.

Where were we? What was I again?

Shy looks at the way the face widens out, pulled back towards the empty eyeholes, then down to a strange wet bump above the snarl where there must've been a snout or a nose, human nose, plastic surgery, removable parts of plastic potato-heads and half-remembered scenes in forbidden films.

The bigger one has come to rest against the smaller one, both of them with their little arms and legs perked up, frozen ready, facing the disembodied parent high above the pond like mid-tickle puppies, waiting. He wonders about the insides. There's no way of knowing without touching them, lifting them up. If he stabbed them would they just collapse in on themselves, wheeze-releasing a nasty gas, or would they explode, showering him with old brown blood or piss or pondwater or whatever's swilling about in their bloated guts? The thought fills his mouth with sicky burp and he retches, acid belch, pondwater swill, tight as a drum, shrivelled anus, bag of bile, fatty hard overdone burger flesh with teeth and striped . . . BADGERS.

Fucking Get In.

Finally!

Bloated dead badgers.

He drops his stick.

He whacks the water either side of him, two hard flat slaps, and a bird squacks and panics up into the sky from behind him.

The badgers stay where they are.

He wipes his nose on his wet sleeve, sniffs and spits.

He speaks to them.

Are you a Mr and Mrs, then, are you?

Fuuuuuuck's sake, he whines into his sleeve. Someone killed you?

You're so *gross*.

He breathes and sighs and stares up at the dimpled sky. The clouds are coagulated into rutted clusters, backlit by the stubborn moon.

What are you doing in here, all puffed up? Floating. What's going on?

He speaks gently to the badgers in his young voice, no swagger, no affected patois, no pretence, like he'd talk to his mum before, before everything became a fight. A scared boy with two dead bodies, beyond recognition.

Did someone do something to you? A human? How did you die?

He hugs himself. Stuttering. Whimpering.

Urrgh. Where's your hair gone?

'I was in a long dark tunnel', he says, sadly. Do you know that tune? Valley of the Shadows? I want it played at my funeral.

'Felt that I was in this long   dark   tunnel', he says again.

It's a sample. It's from one of my favourite tunes.

No. The badgers don't know that tune.

He cries a whingeing groan and hangs his head. Snotty. Half-sunk. Confused.

At least they're together. Maybe they died of the same illness, or came here together to end whatever badger hassles they'd been going through.

He feels colossally sad.

Blisteringly sad.

Almost ecstatically sad.

He walks slowly out of the water. He squelches and sloshes over to his backpack and hauls it on.

He picks up his Walkman and carries it on his open palm to stop it getting dripped on.

He walks to the other side of the reeds to check on the badgers. They're still there.

He crosses the track, back up towards the house.

He smells of pond. Everything smells of pond. He feels like he could sniff his way into individual microbes, earthy worming growgreen liquid stink, newts and shoots, silty, fruity, and as he walks he gathers in the smell of dry leaves, crinkly things, brown oily smells, good rot, herby hydro deep woodlousey sticky mushroomy smells, things turning, things that go on smelling this way whether or not a wet teenager is here to smell them. He is all sense. He isn't having any thoughts, he's all smell and shadows and ruined trainers, a frighteningly awake sleep creature sloshing along.

Something is cronking, ribbering quietly near him. Above or below him. Something else is fidgeting. Something is flapping. There's a *coo, coo*. It's all happening now. He doesn't recognise his brightening senses. The badgers have fused his system, or maybe he's just knackered and mad. He trips and stumbles on unexpected soft bits and bumps, like a kerb-wobble drunk. He plods on, bursting empty.

He could learn to speak this language: night-end. He could train his indoor pupils to permanently widen, to drink it in.

Strange dizzy wake-up. Untangling.

He breathes deeply and it's clean digestible air. He feels it hitting his insides.

He asks himself the question Jenny always starts with:

What's happening with Shy this week?

Well, I went down to the pond. There were these badgers and . . . umm, I'm heading back now. Back up to the house.

And how are you feeling about that? About the night?

Umm.

Take your time.

I feel kind of lonely. Bit embarrassed and sad, if I'm honest, Jenny. A bit scared.

Oh Shy, he says, in Jenny's gentle voice. Bad luck.

He wants to know what happened to those badgers. He wants someone to explain it.

He wants a cigarette. He wants to get into his pyjamas and go to sleep.

He's so, so tired.

He wants to stop having ups and downs. He wants to stop his mind. Shut it off. He wants to sleep for days and days and have no dreams. He wants to be eighteen, able to go to an offie and buy a bottle of Captain Morgan and a pack of fags and go and sit somewhere all alone and not think.

He wants his mum to drive him to Harvester for an All You Can Eat Buffet and bottomless Coke and ice cream factory and there be no trouble or special event or birthday pressure, just a treat. Just the two of them.

He wants to put the rucksack down.

He wants the V Recordings logo tattooed on his arm.

He wants Marmite soldiers dipped in a runny egg.

He wants Technics turntables.

He wants a car.

He wants a girlfriend who could visit him at weekends and get off with him all afternoon and transfer the taste of her strawberry lip balm to his lips.

He wants to be able to tune in to pirate radio but he's living in this shite old mansion converted into a school for badly behaved boys in the middle of bumblefuck nowhere.

He wants to be taller.

He wants some facial hair.

The birds have started singing and individual trees and bushes are emerging from the sameness of the night.

He wants to win the lottery and buy the house for Steve and the staff so they can keep on running Last Chance. Knock through the ground floor and make a studio. A wall of speakers where the lockers are.

The house is looking pale and spooky in the almost-dawn, hunched over the garden like a chunk of grumpy history.

Shy plods sniffling up the lower lawn towards the ha-ha.

The sky is brightening, warming pinkish and soft. It could almost be evening, it makes Shy feel cosy and invited, ten years old, allowed to stay up late because his mum and Iain have got friends over, might be allowed in the garden in his PJs, might be allowed a sip of Iain's beer.

The stone walls of the house come to life, glowing slabs of butter light, cut into clean lines, with fancy carved windows and special chimneys. They've been taught about the architect, taught about the ghosts and the visits from kings, but how in ever-loving fuck do they cut the stones so neat, stack them, curve and carve and keep them solid for hundreds of years, how do they glue it all together? He needs to find out. If he was abducted by aliens, if they touched down soft and silent on the lawn now and hoovered him into their spaceship, how would he fare with a basic set of queries? He'd be a let-down. *Show us fire*, they'd say. *Share the secrets of electricity, bombs, faxes, flight.* He'd be guessing, struggling to remember. I can tell you about the music I love, how it came to be, I can tell you about acid house, hardcore, dancehall and hip-hop, but the aliens would have shoved him out, plop down onto the lawn with a damp thud, bugger-all use, waste of space.

How strange, they'd say, *some among them do not have any knowledge whatsoever.*

He clambers up over the ha-ha and lies on his side. He puts his Walkman on the grass. He slips out of the straps of his rucksack and rolls over, spreadeagled in the nearly-day, shivering.

He thinks of the badgers, floating by the reeds, drifting in and out of contact with each other, softly bumping. He thinks of them woken up, clambering awkwardly out of the pond, trot-pottering along, following his scent. Tricky to leathery-waddle on their shrunken legs, thick dead claws brittle and decayed, past their sell-by date, whiskers long gone, rotten but determined, follow the wet human, up through the field, heigh-ho, wait up Shy, through the gap in the hedge, it's off to work we go, across the lower garden, there he is, there he is sleeping on the lawn, but we can't get up this wall.

Excuse us, Shy? We can't get up this wall.

It's a ha-ha. That's what it's called. It's designed to stop exactly this.

He would have to reach down and pick them up. He'd keep his body and legs on the lawn and lean down, full stretch, face reddening, and lift them. They wouldn't weigh much. He'd forgive them their appalling appearance, two engorged Halloween hell-pups, a gaswater corpse couple, and he would help them onto the lawn and they'd lie next to him, frozen snarls grinning up at the sky, watching it turn from hazy beige to clear blue, breathing and watching and being with him.

Ah, that's better. Thanks, Shy.

He smiles and wishes he had a pack of fags.

I love smoking in the morning. It's the best. You're starting to smell, guys.

Oh dear – sorry, Shy.

He's so cold, lying on the wet grass, soaked to the skin, stinking of pond. He's going to get pneumonia. It doesn't matter.

He likes the imaginary voices he's giving the badgers. A smarmy nasal voice for the larger one, a bit like his old headmaster who used to say his mission was to turn weak boys into strong men. A slightly apologetic and mousy voice for the smaller one, like his mum's sweet needling chat.

We're not really supposed to be out in the daytime. But it's lovely up here, by the house, says the smaller badger.

We should never have left the pond, says the bigger badger.

Fuck's sake, says Shy, laughing at his own weird delirium.

Maybe we're Norns, Shy. Remember? The weird sisters?

Shivering uncontrollably.

Maybe we're spies from the twenty-first century saying Hold on, young'un, you're going to want to see this. There's incredible music coming.

He sits up and looks at the house and rubs his arms. They're all in there. Cosy and dry.

Shy feels peace and warmth towards the sleeping boys. He knows it's an illusion, a symptom of the night, the strong spliff, the pond, his tiredness, but he feels that beyond all the abuse and the flashes of violence and cruelty, they're definitely his mates now. Him and Cal are planning on going to a festival next summer. Him and Benny want to start a label. Atomic Bass Recordings. A mushroom cloud as the logo, a revolving blast in the middle of the sticker. They've done some drawings.

I can't imagine this place as luxury flats, says Shy to the badgers.

Oh yes you can. Course you can.

All those busy lives, behind closed doors. Old house all smart and new. Cut into chunks.

Shy smiles. Maybe he'll call his mum tomorrow. Today. He'll call her today.

You really should, says the larger badger.

He's so sleepy.

It's getting light. The house is soft orange and the low sky is bulging with pink fluff. There's a blue hugeness above him.

Beautiful, says the smaller badger.

Shy lies on his side, curls into a pause on the lawn and closes his eyes.

The badgers show Shy himself, asleep in his room, watched by another, back when it was wider, waking up before the false walls made one room into three, broader dreams, in the sixties, waking up as a girl called Eve who stayed with her rich uncle and aunt who couldn't reach her and didn't try and she tunnelled darker and more stubbornly into her melancholy, grappled with powerful nightmares, watched Shy sleeping, blue devils and multiple wakings, screams from the attic, strange visions of herself as old, waved back warnings, carved her name into the wooden beam above her bed, wore scratchy knitted pullovers to hide herself, made awkward calls to her overseas parents, disembodied voices, strangers with strangled manners and antique morals, Shy feels at home inside her head, livid company, inner grim patter, little cuts on her thighs, can I come in, little knocks on the memory door, on the base of her foot, don't you dare, Up and at 'em, Evie, little cuts on the soft inside of her upper arm, exactly matching, waking up to a man with a face made of sheets and his fingers in her throat, in between her legs curled upwards then painful and shrieking awake in the cold dark house hearing a woman scream in the attic, sure there's a boy muttering in the unkind walls, unsought ghosts, stolen cigarettes, our daughter is evidently deranged, odd wobbling rage, thumping sense of despondency, difficult age, failure, Nanny

would be ashamed, dry mouth with no words, pointless
panoramic no point to Eve in any direction, Shy feels
transcribed, slid sideways, sloppy in comparison, no
real plan, whereas she has a sudden clear ambition
for a neat and hurtful leaving and he feels it, her idea
which grows and gathers shape and seems the only
rejoinder to the problem of herself, Eve fixating on
a shocking scene, the body which would no longer
be her problem, slapping her mother, unwrapping
herself, bringing shame on her family name, sending
an unforgettable picture postcard to her parents, the
pond, the disgraced daughter becoming unspoken,
verboten, kept in letters and whispers and a rose bush
planted in the walled garden, a line in the Bible about
crime, a gesture to the stupid cult of longevity, dreams
of clunk, snap, gasping then gone, whiteout, crack,
wallop then dead, dreams of the willow, Eve in the
gap between branch and ground, immortal, released,
out of her head then slicing into her giddy evening a
brief yearning to be in London, stealing her uncle's
cigarettes, different person in a similar skin swigging
gin from the bottle in the drawing room, singing, dark
outside looking in, any old unknown anyone, spots on
her forehead like Shy, zits, little *Top of the Pops* skits,
muttering Stones lyrics to herself, lost between the
girls at school, the bullies in her head, the matron's
kindness, drink all this gin and swing blue-gone by

the pond and cease pondering, so she plans it, night
after night, feels less alone when she's plotting, waits
for a full moon, stolen gardener's rope coiled cinematic
beneath the bed, replace Daddy's rehashed M. R. James
ghost stories with Eve's homemade horror, serve them
right for leaving, serve her right for caring, escape
her endless unease in the willow tree where she sits
in the hot day feeling lifeless, where she waits for
her thoughts to stop snitching, hearing voices, afraid
of awake, afraid of asleep, creeps out of the room
which used to be Eve's, once upon a time Shy's, the
floorboards complain, stone steps whisper her name,
out of the conservatory window, bag already packed,
Eve be nimble, Eve be quick, jump off the line of the
ha-ha brick, run down the lawn, into the lower garden,
no stranger to night-time adventures, lighter in the run
with no backpack, higher than Shy, sharper than Shy,
more clarity and exactitude in her thoughts, angrier
than Shy, it shocks him to feel it, a lesson and a taste,
Eve out through the echo of the bottom hedge making
haste, she climbs up the willow and gets on with it,
briskly bloody-minded, taught to tie knots by naval-
cold Daddy, taut on the limb of the tree, show a child
affection with technical lessons, Shy feels a pang for
Iain's DIY gestures, weirdly bright night, everything
quiet, straddling the willow's hard-split arm, enjoying
the almost splinters from the petrol-smelly rope, and

then Eve sees two badgers walk towards the tree as Shy
dreams them up and out of the pond, one large, one
smaller, real animals, unrealistic soft and beautiful and
picture-book charming, big and alive from above as
if another person's story has been slid or remembered
into hers, Eve in the eaves looking down on a strange
performance, slightly detached from the human view,
wide-angled, impossible, unsurprised, everyone on
good terms in the thirty-year crease, strange witnesses,
of course we speak languages unknown to us, of course
we speak badger, speak heartsore, huddled beneath her
like sheepdogs, they sniff and peer, then call up at her,
Hello Eve, not tonight, not yet, see Shy, Eve flaps the
rope, she claps, she slaps the tree, she says Piss offffffff,
she says Boo, she says Do go away, she asks Shy Who?,
she laughs in her sleep and wakes up, but they stay,
they pootle about at the base of her world-tree talking
about all the things she doesn't want to miss in the
next few years, the seventies, the music that's coming,
the love, the books, the freedom of movement beyond
the body policed and ill-fitting, the widening of her
life, Shy laughs at the badgers' funny voices, he feels
the bumpy willow bark ridged and indenting their
hands and their legs, feels the soft floor under-paw,
feels how it is to seek and smell as a badger, feels how
it is to try and send a message across a species divide,
it is easy, it is the easiest thing in the whole difficult

world, Eve lies on the branch and listens, resigned to the strange night, this has happened before in the dark, visions only partially hers, intuited, half-imparted, cheek on the bark, she looks over to the pond and can't tell what's in the middle by the little island but it might be a boy, a head-and-shoulders bust, staying still on the surface just watching, cheek on the lawn, cheek on the soft pillow, level with the destination, the decision, and the badgers pootle off chatting amongst themselves of things happening or not happening, and Eve shuffles backwards down the branch to the bulbous trunk, jumps and lands with a heeled thud on the earth, not hanging but landed, and runs a fast loop of the pond to check for a boy drowning but there's nobody, no body, no badgers, no boy, but the running feels good so she does it again, now she's not dead she may as well run as fast as she can, wheeling around the pond, remembering for him, like the trains on a tight track at the steam fair, and she peels off over the dirt road through the dark treeline which bristles crossly as she bursts through it and she runs back to the house, plimsolls sinking in the ploughed mud of the field, and she sprints up through the gap, noisy breath in her head, hammering heart life, stumbles into the lower garden which is brambly and tricky, she trips, she laughs at herself, slips, giddy, what a muddy fool, she's left the rope in the tree, sinister joke, but that's tomorrow's worry, and she runs across the garden and sees a shape on the flat top of the ha-ha, on the neatly striped night-lawn, black and white, tiny beneath the cruel house, it's an animal, it's a dead body, it's a sleeping boy in baggy jeans and a hoodie, soaked, shivering, and next to him is a bag.

She unzips the bag and takes out a stone,

a beautiful wonky flint

and *what*

the fuck

you

are

what

what

the *you little*

you

doing *weirdo?*

fuck are

What the fuck are you doing, you little weirdo?

Shy!

Blinding sky. Weird yellowy burning.

Oi. Come look at this!

Shy sits up as a toilet roll lands with a gentle *plumpf* next to him. Then a CD case breaks nearby. Then another. He looks around, then up at the open windows, wanker signs and blurred faces, middle fingers, shouting. Owen has come to the patio doors. Shy scrabbles around, pats the grass, realises how cold he is, how not-dead he is, how freezing and confused, he can't see properly, his eyes are fuzzy, he's been pulled from his dream too quickly.

Brightness.

Oi DICKHEAD.

A brown apple core hits his chest.

Mentalist.

Why's he wet? Oi Steppa, what you doing?

He stands up, massive headrush, staggering a bit, and squelches to his rucksack. It's no longer night-time, he can trust his eyes. He unzips the main pocket and grabs a flint. The flint is like a little gerbil wearing a white chalky coat, black flesh poking through in places. Cold. Knobbly. Eve's flint. It fits nicely in his hand. He runs a few paces up to the house and chucks it as hard as he can into the central conservatory windows. The window is divided into eight squares and Shy hits the top left panel which pops with a classic tinkling crash and Owen runs yelling back into the dark house, covering his head like a war movie extra, fleeing from a blast.

Shy walks back to the bag and grabs another flint. The boys in the top window are whooping and shouting and swearing and braying. This next flint is like a misshapen carrot, fits in his hand like a bumpy dick, gnarled and cold. He runs a little closer to the house and lobs it up at one of the top attic windows and there's a clinkling patter and a boof, then mad laughter from the boys.

Shy Guy, what the fuck are you on?

Shy runs back to the bag and drags it closer to the house. He grabs two flints, one apple-sized moon, one wedge-shaped torso with its limbs cut off. He chucks one through the far left conservatory window, and one at the dark window he thinks is his own. Back to the bag and not even looking, grabbing flints, breaking windows, underarm lobs for the top windows, overarm flings for the ground floor, the older windows smash like crystal, easy-peasy seventeenth-century-listed squeezy, piece of piss to smash, six windows, seven, got his eye on the far right window which is slightly open, he thinks it's the bathroom, it's so noisy with everyone screaming and shouting and booing and *brap-brap-brapping* him, his breath ragged and noisy, his heart pounding, and he starts to scream, a fully unselfconscious cry, like a baby, pure wailing, like Jenny said. *It might be good for you to go somewhere and shout it out.* He bellows it crackling out, gasps for breath and appraises his work and starts again, hurrying back to the bag, screaming at the shattering gap-toothed face of the monstrous handsome house as he chucks, roaring in tune with the sounds of the breaking panes, and he doesn't notice Owen running full tilt, seventeen stone barrelling across the lawn, and then he is knocked clean off his feet.

Shy briefly flies.

Gotcha.

They land in a painful heap and Owen lies on him, panting.

Bloody Nora, lad.

Shy tries to wriggle but it's hopeless. Thump-thump-thump in his ears, the red heat throbbing rampant in his mind, he cannot move, he is encased in a shower-fresh mound of Owen, solid. He roars one more time, a gravelly rip in his throat, and then he gives up and rests his face in tears and grass and mud and feels Owen's heartbeat drumming on his back like the muffled kick of a distant break.

You're alright, says Owen. *That's enough. You're OK.*

Shy is lying painfully on his arm, clasping a little flint the size of a toy car. Hard and sharp in his hand. He squeezes it. He breathes and Owen talks into the back of his neck:

Alright? I'm going to get up off you now, alright? No moreOooffuckinell . . . There's a whump and a groan and Owen is forced off him and Shy is exposed to the light again, clasping his hot little flint as Owen is buried, kicking and cussing like a bull, under Benny, Jamie and one other Shy can't make out, a tangle of teenage boys, they're rolling and punching and holding Owen's giant tree-trunk legs down and sitting on him and saying *Go Shy*.

Fucking go for it, Shy, says Benny, so Shy jumps up and sees that the lawn is covered with the others, all of them are into his rucksack for flints, and they're all breaking windows. Owen clambers free from his attackers, red and livid, and the boys run off laughing, springing and slapping each other, fresh and excited for violence and play, an out-of-the-ordinary start to the day. There's more shouting from the house, the crack and tinkling splash of broken glass, dull cracks of missed rocks against lead or stone and Riley screaming *Oi fuckoff!* as a flint bounces back and nearly hits him, and Shy just stands

watching,

holding his last stone, his 600-million-year-old toy,

feeling extremely light and blank and empty.

Shy!

Steve and Amanda come running around the side of the house. He feels the old tired flicker in his spirit; trouble up, trouble long, all gone wrong, trouble taking months to fix, trouble for his mum, trouble with the pigs, the all-involved trouble theatre he has to live in again, but Steve doesn't look angry, he looks scared. Amanda is rushing like she's Challenge Anneka, searching for something. Desperate. They ignore the others leaping about, they don't even look at the front of the house. They come straight to him.

Shy, come here.

Amanda gets to him first and pulls him into a hug.
Steve joins and puts his arms around them both. Shy
is in the middle. He clutches his flint, warm in his
clammy palm.

I'm . . .

Shh, Shy.

Fucking hell, mate, says Steve.

They squeeze him.

I'm sorry.

It's a load of old windows, who gives a shit.

I'm sorry.

Honestly, smash every last window if you need to, Shy.

The boys are gathering round, taking the piss, curious,
bashful, *Little man flipped, You alright, dicksplash?*

Chilly lads in their boxers and T-shirts.

Owen comes over and joins them, bleeding from his
chin.

Benny pads across the lawn in his flip-flops and joins
the huddle.

Cal reaches in and puts a hand on Shy's shoulder.

Nobody speaks.

The dangerous young men stand around with the broken Last Chance behind them.

Shy is wrapped up in other people,

no weight on his back,

eyes closed,

waiting for another day.

Typeset by Faber & Faber Limited.
Manufactured by Friesens on acid-free,
100 percent postconsumer wastepaper.